A Cowboy's New Family

SWEET VIEW RANCH
BOOK SEVEN

JESSIE GUSSMAN

Contents

Acknowledgments

Cover art by Julia Gussman
Editing by Heather Hayden
Narration by Jay Dyess
Author Services by CE Author Assistant

Listen to the unabridged audio for FREE performed by Jay Dyess on the Say with Jay channel on YouTube. Get early access to all of Jay's recordings and listen to Jessie's books before they're available to the general public, plus get daily Bible readings by Jay and bonus scenes by becoming a Say with Jay channel member.

Chapter One

Tosha gripped her crying child and looked around the kitchen she'd called home for the last six months.

It wasn't much different than any kitchen she'd cooked in since she'd left her mother's home when she was sixteen. Ratty old linoleum, two cupboard doors were missing, one hung crookedly, the sink leaked, and the stove was minus one heating element. There was no microwave. She'd lived without one more than with, and she tried to tell herself it was better for her children's health that way.

Whether that was true or not, she wasn't entirely sure. She'd seen articles saying it was so, but when a person was trying to find enough money to buy groceries, the cancer-causing elements of microwaves weren't exactly the most important consideration.

The baby in her arms fussed, and she automatically swayed back and forth. After five children, she had been ingrained with the ability to quiet a crying child.

No, she wasn't going to miss this place at all.

Her oldest boy ran through, chasing his younger sister who cried and screamed for her mother. River had a tendency to be dramatic, but Mitchell, her oldest boy, had a tendency to be mean. Tosha always blamed his father for that, but maybe it was the poverty they'd lived in Mitchell's whole life.

A soul-deep tiredness seemed to sap the life out of her, but she couldn't afford to stop and rest. Her grandmother had said she was sending someone to help her move the last of her things out of the house and take her and her children to Gram's house in Sweet Water, North Dakota.

Tosha viewed this as a new start. An opportunity to right the wrongs of her past, chart a new course, and make decisions that were smart and forward-thinking, especially when it came to her children. She hadn't done well by them, and it was time she took control of herself and did what needed to be done even if it was hard, and even if she would rather do something else.

She told herself this as she held out an arm so River could run into it.

"Mitchell is being mean!" her daughter sobbed against her side. Phoenix, her six-month-old, squirmed in her arms, not liking the fact that he no longer had his mother's full attention.

"He just wants you to react. If you ignore him, he'll quit picking on you." Her voice sounded tired, and it lacked the authority she wanted to convey. After all, Mitchell had yet to get tired of picking on anyone, and he seemed to love nothing better than to make someone else cry.

That wasn't to say that Mitchell didn't have a soft heart. He really did. He just seemed to have a split personality. Sometimes he was the sweetest thing, and sometimes Tosha wondered if he could really be her son.

Bailey, her six-year-old, wandered into the room, clutching her dolly to her chest. She hated moving more than all the other kids combined. If nothing else, Tosha hoped this move to her gram's house would be the last move ever, just for Bailey, who longed to have an actual home with roots and neighbors and security. Something Tosha had not been able to give her since her first husband had left when Bailey was less than a week old.

Gemmy, two, waddled into the kitchen, sucking her thumb and dragging a blanket. Even in her short life, she'd moved four times. This scene had to be familiar to her.

At least this time they didn't have to pack up the beds, which were falling apart. Except for Bailey's and River's. Their bed was an old mattress on the floor. Phoenix used a pack and play as his crib, and that had been easy to pack away, even though it was broken and she had to fold the sides carefully to get it to roll up the way it was supposed to.

"When is the man going to be here?" Mitchell asked, standing on the couch and looking out the window down the street. Tosha hadn't even tried to put curtains on the windows. At one point back when she was still young and naive, she'd decorated each house they'd lived in with whatever frilly knickknacks she could scrounge up from the secondhand store or yard sales. But for the last few years, she'd lost any thought of staying in one place long enough to make the effort worth it.

Or maybe trying to keep up with five children, work a job and make enough money to make rent, and worry about when her latest man was going to walk out—they always walked out—had kept her too tired to worry about something so frivolous as home decor. That type of thing was for people who had money and time and help. Or no kids. A faithful husband. A high school diploma.

Her mother had told her one day she'd regret quitting school, but she'd been convinced she was in love and had thought her mother was dead wrong. She'd tell her mother she was right, except she'd died of pancreatic cancer two years prior, so Tosha didn't have a chance.

"Someone is pulling in!" Mitchell announced from his vantage point in the living room.

"What kind of vehicle?" Tosha asked as she held River who still sniffled and Phoenix who was ready to go down for a nap but wasn't going to sleep in this house again.

"An SUV. It's blue." Mitchell could sometimes be difficult, but he was her best helper, too, and she depended on him to help her out more than she should.

Or maybe it was good for children to have some responsibility and feel like they were contributing to the family. She'd read that somewhere, but she couldn't remember where, and she didn't want to mess her kids up any more than what she already had.

Gemmy toddled to the door as Mitchell went to open it.

"Just wait," Tosha said, not sure if the guy her gram was sending to get her had a blue SUV. She pulled her phone out, sending off a one-handed text, while River fussed because she'd let go of her.

Her gram's answer came back right away.

Yes, and he just said he pulled in.

"Hang on, Mitchell," she said, but too late as he'd opened the door while she was looking at her phone and had gone through it, Gemmy waddling after him.

Just how she wanted to meet this dude her gram couldn't say enough good about—chasing her kids, flustered, and more tired than she could ever remember being in her life before.

"Stay here," she commanded River before she hurried out to grab Gemmy, who, despite being female, was the most precocious child she'd had. There wasn't anything that kid hadn't tried, and if there was a way to escape, Gemmy would find it. When she was younger, Tosha had put the pack and play upside down over top of her to keep her from climbing out of it. That had worked until Gemmy had figured out that she could slide it over to the stairs and crawl out from under it. Of course, she'd gone down the stairs head over heels, and Tosha had thought she'd died, but after crying for a couple of minutes, Gemmy had been right as rain. It was Tosha who had taken the rest of the day to recover and who still had nightmares about it.

She'd grabbed Gemmy, glancing up to see the man had gotten out of his SUV. It was a newer model, if she wasn't mistaken, and it looked clean and shiny. Way too nice for her ragtag family.

Gemmy resisted being picked up and started screaming in protest as Tosha held her around the waist, trying to keep a hold of Phoenix who was fussy because he should have been sleeping and was missing his naptime.

She struggled to balance both kids and almost plunged headfirst down the two steps to the sidewalk. If Sioux City had a bad part of town, this was it.

But the man looked tall and strong and capable. Not the kind of man who had ever looked twice at her, although she'd definitely looked more than once at guys like him. If she had waited, like her mother had told her to, for someone like him to come along, would he have been interested?

It didn't matter. She reminded herself that one of the things she had committed to when she'd decided to change her life was that she was not interested in men. Not even a little. She'd had terrible luck with them, picking cheaters and liars and lazy bums with a certainty that gamblers would envy.

Still, she wasn't going to be rude. Gemmy continued to cry. The man stopped in front of her and held out his hand.

"You must be Tosha Wells. I'm Tobias Clybourn. Your gram sent me to pick you up."

Her hand slipped into his. It was rough and hard and felt like it knew how to work. His face seemed serious, but those deep blue eyes also held compassion and, not pity, but maybe understanding. Or maybe she wanted that so much she conjured it up.

Regardless, she was so taken aback, it took her a bit to answer. Before she could open her mouth, she saw movement behind the man's head, and in the next split second, she realized that her son had jumped into his SUV and started driving it down the street.

Chapter Two

Tobias wasn't sure exactly what he was expecting when he'd told Mrs. Wells that he'd pick up her granddaughter. He'd known she was in dire straits, and he'd also known that he might be proposing marriage to her, just because of the promise he'd made to Mrs. Wells and the letter he'd gotten in the mail not long ago.

He supposed he'd expected a woman who looked like her best years were behind her, slightly chunky with gray-streaked hair and stained and ratty clothes.

The stained and ratty clothes were evident, but the woman with the sweet brown eyes, dark brown hair, and full red lips didn't resemble the rest of his speculation at all. Not even a little.

Beautiful might have been a bit of an exaggeration, just because she looked like she hadn't slept in months, but she was definitely on the sweet side of pretty, and he found himself staring at her. Maybe he was also thinking that he'd planned to propose a marriage of convenience to her and was trying to reconcile the woman in front of him with the woman he'd thought he'd be marrying.

But he hadn't gotten anything more than an introduction out of his mouth before the woman screamed and shouted, "Mitchell, get back here!"

To Tobias's surprise, she ran past him, continuing to scream.

Tobias turned to see what the cause of her dismay could be and realized his vehicle was going down the street without him.

Mitchell must be the name of the boy in the driver's seat, his head barely visible as Tobias sprinted past the woman.

"I'll get him," he shouted as he pushed himself to go as fast as he could. The car wasn't going very fast, but if the kid crashed it, at the least it would mean they didn't make it back to North Dakota tomorrow like he'd planned. At worst, someone could be hurt or killed.

The trip would be too much for five kids to do all at once, so Tobias had planned on stopping. He had some nieces and nephews, so he wasn't totally ignorant when it came to young children.

Thankfully, the kid seemed to mix up the gas pedal with the brake, and Tobias was able to reach the door, yanking on the handle.

It was locked.

Figures. A safety feature designed by engineers who no doubt had never had children. Not that Tobias could talk, although he felt like he might be baptized with fire if this was the way things started.

He slapped the window, jogging along beside the car.

"Let me in," he called.

The kid looked over, smiling, but his eyes wide, like he was terrified, too.

He made no move to unlock the doors.

If Tobias had a second to think, he might have been annoyed with himself for leaving the keys in his vehicle, but in Sweet Water where he lived, no one locked their car, especially if they weren't planning on leaving it for any length of time.

A stop sign loomed large ahead, and Tobias slapped on the window again.

"Let me in," he said. Then, in a moment of what he later considered to be pure brilliance, he added, "Please!"

The magic word at any age, he supposed, as the kid reached over and hit the button for the window.

Tobias did not hesitate, just in case the kid changed his mind, but threw himself into the window, shoving the kid aside and reaching with his hand for the brake.

It took about two seconds for him to stop the car, then he put it in park, hit the button to turn the motor off, and grabbed the key from where he'd set it in the console.

He took a minute to catch his breath and thank the Lord there hadn't been an accident before he shoved back out of the window.

"I shouldn't have rolled down the window," the kid muttered.

Really? That was how the kid reacted? If he'd done something like that when he was little, his parents would have made sure he didn't do it again by making the punishment worse than the pleasure of the joyride.

But this was not his kid—yet—and from what Tobias knew, the kid had been through a good bit more than Tobias at this age. Not that Tobias hadn't had his share of trials and heartache. Just not when he was this young.

"You enjoy driving?" he said, just because he wanted to develop a relationship with these kids, regardless of what their mother decided to do when he made his offer to her.

"Knew I would," the kid said, not looking the slightest bit remorseful.

"There are lots of wide-open spaces in North Dakota where you can practice driving, but not if you're going to do it when you don't have permission," he said, his words easy and censure-free. He didn't know if he should handle this with more force and anger, but he'd never seen anger have good long-term consequences. Plus, as a rule, he didn't get angry. He'd worked on that part of his personality for a long time now and hadn't arrived, exactly, but had definitely gotten better.

It seemed the patience he'd worked for might be needed with this child.

"I'm so sorry!" The woman who'd met him in front of her door had run down the street behind him, her two small children in both arms, panting, her face red. "I can't believe he did that!"

Then her attention turned to the kid in the front seat of Tobias's car. "Mitchell George Patton Wells, what in the world were you thinking?" Her voice sounded stern and firm, although it didn't seem like she was angry either.

He appreciated the fact that she could be firm with her children without anger, although how a mother could not be angry over what her kid had just done was beyond Tobias's comprehension.

This could be his new family.

Even worse, this kid could be his responsibility.

Lord? I feel like I'm following You, but are You really leading me in this direction?

He knew he shouldn't question the Lord. No one should. When God gave commands, a person's responsibility was to just blindly follow, not look around to see if there wasn't a better way.

Doubting himself was something that anyone might do. Tobias was not immune. Although, he normally felt like he had a pretty good handle on his relationship with the Lord and on knowing what God wanted. Even if sometimes it seemed rather out there to him.

He was definitely not saying that he had a good handle on his spiritual life. He could see a lot of room for growth. In fact, the closer he got to the Lord, the more room for growth he could see.

The woman berated her child a little bit more, who didn't seem the slightest bit remorseful.

On the one hand, Tobias would like to grab the little punk by the neck. On the other, he imagined it was probably some kind of defensive mechanism the kid had developed in order to survive the life he'd been born into. Tobias suspected the woman figured the same. She seemed old and tired and beaten down.

He hadn't seen a picture of her at all, and he had expected someone older, since she did have five children.

A little curl of something went through his stomach, anxiety maybe? Marriage was a lifetime commitment, and he had already promised the Lord he would make it, but he knew that it probably wasn't going to be sugarplums and rose drops, but rather a life like Hosea's in the Bible.

Normally he would never recommend someone marry a person without knowing them and especially without knowing what kind of spiritual life they had, but without even meeting this woman, he had felt God urging him to do something beyond the normal every time Mrs. Wells talked about her granddaughter, Tosha, and her five children.

"I really am sorry," Tosha said as she straightened, still holding two children in her hands, her face red, her forehead dotted with sweat.

"I'll take one of those kids if you want me to," he offered, knowing that she probably would refuse. What woman was going to hand her children off to a stranger?

"Are you the man my grandmother sent to help me move?" she asked, seeming to ignore his question.

He nodded his head. "We talked about it, and I told her that I would give you a hand moving." He had told her that he would help her in other ways too, and had gone so far as to tell Mrs. Wells that he was going to propose marriage to her granddaughter. How did a man do that anyway? He'd never been close to proposing marriage, although he'd been in a relationship where he thought that marriage was going to be the end result.

A shot of pain clutched around his ribs, and he pushed that thought aside. He wasn't going to think about that; he'd put that behind him forever.

"All right then. If you want to hold one of the children, you can. She said you were a good man." She sighed. Then she smiled appreciatively. "I'm sorry. That made it sound like I was allowing you to hold my child. I really appreciate your offer. I am used to holding children but not used to running down the street with them."

Two cars had chugged by slowly through the narrow street, and Tobias could see several neighbors looking curiously off porches, two of them holding children and two of them old enough to be retired with a whole bunch of nursing home brochures sitting on their kitchen table.

"I understood," he said easily. He didn't know what else to say. He had never been much of a talker. He always allowed his actions to speak for him. But somehow he was going to have to find words to ask this woman to do something that he knew God wanted him to do. Of course, if he asked and she said no, he supposed that let him off the hook, didn't it?

He would have to talk to the Lord about that later. He hadn't considered questioning that when God first prompted him.

It wasn't too late to back out, and while Tobias would have easily said that he would do whatever God wanted him to do, he felt himself getting cold feet about this.

"She's probably going to cry, but my arms are killing me," the woman said.

"You're Tosha?" he asked, knowing she'd not argued with him when he'd called her by name before, but figuring he ought to know her name and make sure he was with the right woman.

"Yes. Tosha Wells," she said, pausing a bit before the "Wells." That wasn't her actual name, as far as Tobias knew. He thought she'd been married several times, and...she'd lived with a man or two.

He'd always thought when he got married it would be to someone just as pure as he was. There was a part of him that still wanted that. Still wanted someone to be completely and totally devoted to just him. The way he would be to his wife. He figured most Christian men felt the same way.

"I'm sorry, in the chaos I missed your name."

"I'm Tobias Clybourn," he said, using both hands to take the little girl she held out to him, who, when she realized what they were trying to do, tried to cling to her mother.

"I'll be right here, Gemmy. I'm not going to leave you," Tosha said.

He liked her name. Tosha. It had seemed odd and a little foreign to him at first, but he liked that it seemed to be a bit sassy but still sweet and unique. Unique the way she was unique. He had to try to think of good things, because otherwise, he would be bogged down with the idea that he was getting himself into something that he would never be able to get himself out of and he could end up regretting for the rest of his life.

But a man never regretted following the Lord, did he?

He thought he'd had a strong faith, but all of these questions seemed to be battering at it. Did he really have a strong enough faith to do something so...crazy?

"That's Gemmy," Tosha said, just in case he hadn't heard her use her name earlier.

"I thought so. That's an interesting name. Not one I've heard before." He was terrible at making small talk. He wanted to just get to the meat of the matter, ask her to marry him, tell her that he was here to…rescue her? He didn't think women wanted to be rescued anymore, although that didn't keep men from wanting to do the rescuing. He supposed he'd seen a lot of men who were just as happy to not have any responsibility and to only live for themselves.

He couldn't seem to shake the desire to want to protect and provide, whether it was for his own family on the Sweet View Ranch his family owned, or whether it was for this single mom and her five kids, who desperately needed someone to be a strong and steady influence in her life.

Lord, I could be a strong and steady influence without having to marry her.

The silence rang loud, and he knew that was because God had already told him what to do. And God probably wasn't going to argue with him or discuss it. Even though Tobias, who didn't normally feel like he needed to discuss much of anything, desperately longed to discuss this and to come to a different conclusion.

"Mitchell, you come with me. We're going back to the house." The woman's voice was firm, and she didn't give the boy any room for argument.

"It's not far, but you can sit in the car and I can give you a ride," he said. Somehow he had forgotten about his car in all of the things that he'd been thinking. Probably his nervousness on knowing that within the next few days, he intended to ask this woman to marry him.

He could court her. Try to convince her, but he didn't want to pretend to love her and to feed her a line of baloney. He wanted to be straight up with her. That was his personality.

"Oh. I forgot about the car. Okay. I guess… Can we all get in it?" she asked him, lifting her brows.

"Sure. Everyone should fit. I traded my pickup in for it, on purpose." He clamped his mouth shut as her eyes opened wide.

"On purpose?" she asked, echoing the words he shouldn't have said.

"Yeah," he said, not saying anything more. She didn't need to know, at least not right now, that he had been thinking that he was going to need a vehicle that would haul around a woman and her five children. If he was going to ask Tosha to marry him.

That was information that he could wait to talk about.

She let it go, thankfully. All the kids climbed in the car with them, and he started out down the street, intending to drive around the block. The woman sat beside him in the passenger seat, holding her baby, and seemed to be a little worried.

"Something wrong?" he asked as he checked his mirrors and then started driving.

"Not really. I just know I shouldn't be holding the baby in the front seat. They should be in car seats and all that, but...it is less than a block from our house, and it's so nice to sit down."

"It's not far. I suppose we'd get in just as much trouble as we would if we took a cross-country trip this way, but hopefully nothing will happen between here and there."

And hopefully that would be the way their lives would go, calm and uneventful. Something told him that was wishful thinking.

Chapter Three

Tosha sat in the front seat of Tobias's SUV. She'd been flustered by the man. And she hadn't thought that men could fluster her at all anymore. She thought she had seen and done it all. But she wasn't used to having a man who was obviously respectable paying any kind of attention to her, nor was she used to seeing her sweet little girl being held in such a man's strong arms.

She didn't know where her grandmother had found this man, but if this was the way they grew them in North Dakota... No. She had sworn off men, sworn off having anything to do with them. Didn't she have five children to prove that she was a terrible judge of character and even worse at having any kind of self-control? Not to mention good judgment.

She couldn't blame it all on the men she had been with, although she could blame them not sticking around on their lack of morals and character. But she was turning over a new leaf. She was not doing the falling in love and having gushy feelings for a man. That was a thing of the past. It had led her down all these wrong roads, caused her to make terrible decisions, and caused her to create a life for her kids that was an absolute living nightmare. She couldn't blame Mitchell for wanting to drive a car down the street. She wanted to escape sometimes too.

Although she didn't think her seven-year-old was escaping. He was just being ornery. Maybe trying to get attention. After all, he had four siblings, and she often depended on him to be the responsible one.

Not that he stepped up that much. He was much more likely to make his siblings cry than he was to be stepping up and helping his mother.

"Do you have a lot of things to put in the car?" Tobias asked as he pulled in in front of her house.

She breathed a silent sigh of relief. They'd made it back safely. She shouldn't get in the car with her children not in car seats. She made so many bad decisions that had affected them, she was afraid that was going to be one more. But in her defense, at least she was thinking about her children. Back when she had first had Mitchell and Bailey, she thought more about herself than her children. Thinking about what men thought of her and how to keep her husband, who had ended up leaving anyway. And then how to find another man. The idea of not being attractive and appealing to men was devastating. After all, she didn't want to lose her youthful looks and end up alone and old.

That had led her to living with River and Gemmy's dad and then Phoenix's dad too.

They each moved in long enough to get her pregnant, and then they kicked her out.

Every time she landed on her face, she swore she wouldn't allow it to happen again, but this time, she was serious.

"Take your time," the man said, still sitting at the wheel and waiting for her to answer.

She shook her head. "I'm sorry. There's not much. I got sidetracked by thinking about something else. We just have some bags of clothes, the pack and play, and I have a mattress I'd like to take, but it's not going to fit in this."

"I hired a moving van to take the stuff we can't get in the car. Did your grandma tell you?"

The man's voice was soft and low, soothing. It was the kind of voice she could fall asleep too, wake up to.

But no. She wasn't doing that again. She wasn't going to think about his voice or anything else, other than what was best for her children and her survival. Although, the best thing for her children was to spend as much time as possible around a man like this.

"A moving van? No. Gram didn't say anything about that."

"It should be here any minute," the man said. The words were no sooner out of his mouth than a van pulled up and double-parked on the street beside them.

"Now you're parked in," she said, chewing her lip.

"It's okay. We can direct the movers to get the things you need, and we'll have them move so we can get out. I'm sure they're not going to turn down our spot, right in front of your house."

He didn't say "right in front of your dump," which would have been more accurate. None of the houses on the street looked like they would pass any kind of serious inspection, and hers was the worst of all. From what she understood, it had been a drug house before she moved in. The previous owner had been shot on the porch, along with his girlfriend and the two girls he'd been pimping.

She'd been told that was why the rent was so cheap.

"Wait. You hired movers?" She was determined she wasn't going to depend on any man. She wasn't going to be beholden to anyone, and she wasn't going to fall under anyone's spell. What was this man trying to do?

"I did." The man just stood there looking at her, his eyes hooded, his face serious.

"I can't accept that," she said, the words forced out of her throat. She wasn't going to allow this man to hire movers for her. That was expensive. She knew, because she'd looked into it. On the off chance that she'd find something that she could afford. There was nothing, and she had looked. Hard.

"All right," the man said. "If you don't want movers, I can tell them to go home, and I'll come back and get a U-Haul to bring your things. How soon do you have to have them out of the house?"

She stared at him, ignoring her kids in the back seat who were asking if they could get out.

"By the end of the month," she said absentmindedly, trying to process. Then, she decided she just might as well be blunt. "What are you getting out of this? Is my gram paying you?"

"No," he said, then he looked at the dash and looked back at her. "Is it so hard to believe that I might be doing it just to be nice?"

"Yes. In my experience, men don't do anything just to be nice, without wanting something in return." She glanced back at her children. She wasn't going to go into more detail in front of them. They had been sheltered from most of the terrible things. Although, some of the men that she'd been with had watched TV shows that she would never have allowed her young children to set eyes on, if it had been up to her. She supposed her children hadn't been sheltered as much as what she wanted them to be. For sure.

"Well, I guess every day you get some new experiences."

Really? That was all he was going to say?

"Do you want me to tell the movers to go home?" he asked as movement behind him caught her eye. It was one of the movers from the van waiting to ask if that was the right house, wanting to know if they could get started.

"They're here. They might as well do it. But if you're expecting me to pay with...anything other than money, you can think again." There. She wasn't going to say "sex" in front of her children, but that's what she meant.

The man's eyes narrowed and a look of confusion crossed his face before he seemed...revolted by the idea.

"I'm not asking for any kind of payment. Nothing," he said firmly, as though making sure she knew that he didn't find her the slightest bit attractive.

When she was younger, that would have been devastating. What did she have if she didn't have her looks? But now... She knew she should feel relief, but she felt a little insulted. Of course, she had five children. What man was going to find her attractive if he knew that? And this man didn't just know she had five kids, he seemed to know that she was in dire straits and was here to help her, so he probably pitied her if anything. Although, she felt more like he was disgusted by her.

"All right," she said, lifting her shoulder and yanking on the latch. She would go in and gather her things up, get her children settled in the car, and they would go to her grandma's house. Then this man would leave, and she would never see him again.

Chapter Four

"Are you going to live here?" Bailey asked as Tobias followed Tosha into the house.

Tosha listened to her daughter ask the question and wanted to sink through the floor. Like every man who came around ended up moving in.

Unfortunately, that was closer to the truth than she wanted it to be. After all, she'd lived with four different men in her lifetime and had been married to two. Talk about a lot of mistakes.

"No. We're all moving to North Dakota."

We? She wanted to turn around and jump him about that, but she had to focus. Her first priority was to make sure that she got everything of the children's into the car. After that, she could think about the things the man was saying. After all, he wasn't moving anywhere with them.

"These things need to go out. Each of the children have a bag of clothes. I need to get the pack and play. And I think the movers can bring everything else."

"They're going to be a little bit slower than what we are, probably."

"That's fine. There's nothing left that can't wait a day or two. I really wasn't expecting to be able to bring everything."

"If there's anything you want to leave behind, that's fine too. I know your gram has some things already set up."

"I've talked to her. I know what she has." She didn't mean to be short, but it was weird that this man seemed to know so much about her when she had no clue about him. What was her gram thinking? She really wanted to call and give her an earful. How dare she send this man who seemed to know everything about her to pick her up, when she knew nothing about him? It didn't seem fair. Or right.

Regardless, she focused on getting each child to make sure they had their bag of things, and they each had a little travel pack. They were just in plastic department store bags, but still, she wanted them to have something to occupy themselves on the trip home. She assumed the man was probably going to drive straight through, especially since he said that they would be faster than the movers. If they ended up sleeping in the car, the kids all had a blanket and a few little snacks.

She made sure she had formula for Phoenix and lots of diapers and wipes and several changes of outfits. He was the most difficult one. Not to mention, he was the one who made it exceptionally hard to try to pack, since she had to do everything with the baby on her hip, which meant she was lugging around an extra twenty pounds while doing everything with one hand.

Her back hurt, and her feet were tired, but she tried to ignore all of that while she finished walking through the house and gathering up the children.

Tobias was helpful, and she resented that. Even though she knew she should be grateful for it. She wasn't used to having anyone help her when it was time to go. Usually it was time to move when the man she was with had decided to break up with her and kicked her out.

"All right. Let's carry all of this stuff out to the car," she said to her children, who had been wandering around, more or less in her vicinity. She wanted to make sure that they each had their bag of clothes and their little travel bag.

"The bigger bags of clothes can go in the back. The smaller bags the kids are carrying are bags of things to keep them entertained while we're driving."

Tobias nodded and seemed like it didn't bother him at all that

Gemmy was still in his arms. Once she'd gotten used to the man, she hadn't minded him carrying her around.

River had been up and down and was currently up, so Tobias held out a hand. "I can carry those bags."

She wanted to refuse and do it herself, but instead she said, "I'd appreciate it. I got the car seats out here on the porch, and we can put them in the car, and the kids will be fine for a while."

Her arms would have a chance to take a break.

He jerked his head, then carried the bags to the back of the SUV before he came back and asked which car seat was River's.

She hadn't made it the whole way out of the house, because Mitchell was arguing about wanting to take two bags instead of just one.

She had won the argument, and Mitchell stomped down the steps, unhappy that he didn't get his way, when Tobias asked about River's car seat.

"It's a booster seat right there," she said, pointing out River's seat.

"This one goes in too?" he asked, pointing to Gemmy's seat.

"Yes. And I'll get Phoenix in his car seat." He was still in a baby carrier, and she should have put him in long ago, but she felt bad that he would be in the car seat for so many hours and wanted to keep him out of it as long as possible.

Finally, they were all packed with the kids in their car seats, and she closed the door.

Tobias went to talk to the movers, and she assumed he was telling them what she'd said, which was to leave the furniture, but just bring the bed and the boxes of food and clothes that she had packed upstairs and down.

"Would you like to take one last walk-through?" Tobias asked as she realized she had been standing with her hand on the doorknob, staring back at the house.

"No." She didn't elaborate. While she held some sentimental feelings toward every house she lived in, because it had sheltered her family, she couldn't say that she wasn't happy to leave. Her gram might not have a whole lot of money, but raising her children on the farm outside of Sweet Water, North Dakota, would be far better for them than living in a house like this, here.

"All right, if you're sure you have everything?" He kind of allowed the question to trail off, and she looked back at him, barely able to see him over the top of the vehicle.

"As long as I have all my children, I've got everything I need." She didn't need a man, and maybe that was what she was saying, although she highly doubted that he understood. He thought she was talking about material things, and that was true too. But she didn't need, or want, a man in her life, and she was probably saying that more for herself than him. After all, he had been nothing but completely polite to her. He hadn't been exceptionally forward in any way, nor had he flirted at all. He'd been very reserved and serious. He couldn't have said more loudly if he had shouted at her that he didn't find her attractive and wasn't the slightest bit interested in her.

And again, she wanted that to be okay. She didn't want to be hurt by that or to wish that it were different. After all, this was her new life, and it didn't include men.

"All right then. I'd like to make it halfway there before we stop for the night."

"We're stopping?" she said, unable to keep the surprise out of her voice.

"Sure. We can't have five kids riding in the car that long. They're going to need to get out, right?"

"Yeah, but..." Could she say she wasn't expecting him to be that thoughtful? That she figured she was going to have clothes to change, because most men she knew didn't want to be bothered by the inconvenience of stopping for a child to go to the bathroom.

"But what?" he asked, seeming truly interested in her answer. She wasn't used to that either. Usually men grunted, and expected her to know what they meant, and didn't really give a flip if she had a different idea.

She should give this man the benefit of the doubt, but all of her experience said that was the way men were.

"Nothing. Yes. Thank you." Then she took a breath. "But I can't pay."

She might as well be up-front. Although, she had already told the man she wasn't paying with anything but cash. Unfortunately, she had neglected to mention that she didn't actually have any cash.

"And I'm not paying—"

The man put a hand up. "I'm not asking you to pay. Not with anything." He said that, giving her a look that seemed to be searching her face, making sure she understood exactly what he was saying. Since she had been so careful to make sure he understood what she was saying.

"All right," she said, feeling like all the air went out of her, leaving her limp. This man really wasn't expecting payment? But she knew from experience that men often didn't say what they meant. Maybe later he would change his mind and expect her to pay with whatever she had, although he had been very clear about not finding her attractive.

"All right. Before we get in the car, tell me how long I can expect to go before I need to stop for the kids."

"I try to stop every two hours when I do something, but I know it's a long ride, and stopping that often is hard."

"Will you be able to feed the baby while he's riding in the car seat?"

"I'll get Mitchell to do it. That's why I put Mitchell beside him."

"If he doesn't run off with the bottle," the man said, and Tosha blinked. Was he making a joke? That was the first time that he'd said something that might be remotely considered funny. He certainly hadn't cracked a smile.

He seemed respectable, like she had thought earlier, but also very taciturn and serious. He could definitely use a little light in his life, and with that thought, she considered that maybe she could do something for him. After all, her sense of humor was one of the only things that had gotten her through so many hard times. Maybe she could make this man laugh.

As soon as she thought that though, she pushed the thought aside. Most of the time, men weren't interested in laughing with her. They were interested in other things. And when she wasn't interested in those things, they soon lost interest in her. She had shoved her sense of humor aside when she was in the presence of men.

"All right, you'll let me know if we need to stop. Okay?" the man asked, seeming to want to get this settled between them before they opened the doors and had every word heard by her five children.

"I will."

"And I'll listen." Maybe it was her imagination, but it seemed like possibly one side of his lips quirked up at that. Like he was making a joke.

"I think you have a sense of humor. But you're just really good at hiding it," she said. And with that, she opened her door and got in the car.

Chapter Five

"I have to pee." Bailey's voice came from the back seat.

"How soon are we going to get there?" River whined.

Gemmy was asleep, but Phoenix was up and fussing, and Tosha figured that she ought to make him a bottle.

"It's been four hours. We can stop." Tobias looked at her.

"If you don't mind?"

"I just saw a sign that there was a rest area right up ahead." Tobias nodded and then looked back at the road. Like that was the end of the discussion. Any time she ever traveled with anyone else, it was like pulling teeth to get them to stop for the kids. The fact that they'd been able to go for four hours might have been a mitigating factor, but still, usually it was a fight, like do they really have to go to the bathroom? Like the man didn't have to go to the bathroom, so why should the kids.

She wanted to thank Tobias for being willing to stop the first time one of her kids asked. It was kind of amazing that they had been able to make it so long, but probably the longer they traveled, the more often the kids would want to stop. Still, she wanted to thank him, but as she looked at the strong outline of his face, she swallowed the words.

She hadn't figured out what his deal was. Her gram didn't have a whole lot of money, but she must be paying him. Why else would he be here, picking up a woman he didn't know along with her five children?

Unless he was expecting something from her, but then he saw her and decided from the way she looked that she didn't have anything he would want.

Which was a good thing, she tried to tell herself. She didn't want to have to fend off those kinds of advances.

Sure enough, they came upon a rest area, and Tobias put on his turn signal.

She would be happy to get out and stretch her legs, but most of the stop would be spent taking care of her children.

"I'd like a few words with you if you don't mind, once we're out." Tobias looked over at her, and she assumed that he meant without the children.

"We'll have them play somewhere where there is some open area and not too many people. That should give us some space." She didn't want to say that they needed privacy, because Mitchell was old enough to know that meant that a really interesting conversation was going to happen and he should do his best to hang out and make sure he was there for it.

Tobias pulled in on the far side of the building, making sure that there were no cars on either side of their spot. Even though the rest area was semi-busy, there were plenty of spots, and whether he intended it to be that way or not, Tosha appreciated the fact that she wouldn't have to be super careful that her kids didn't smack a car door into someone else's car or get run over.

"I want you guys all to stay with me. These are the kinds of places where someone might try to take you, and they won't do that if you're near me."

"Or me," Tobias added, and her head jerked toward him.

He had his brows lifted in question, although his words had come out confident and firm.

"Or Mr. Tobias," she added.

"I'll go to the bathroom with him. I don't want to go to the girls' bathroom."

She had looked away from Tobias as Mitchell piped up. Now she spoke low. "Normally I make him go in with me. I... I've heard that child predators sometimes hang out in men's restrooms waiting for boys whose mothers can't accompany them in to take them, and..."

"I've got it," he said, his voice low. Then he raised his gaze and looked in the rearview mirror. She supposed he was meeting Mitchell's eyes. "You can go in with me."

"I hate the girls' restroom. Such a sissy place." Mitchell sneered at Bailey, whose face crumpled, and she started to cry.

Bailey really needed to get a bit of a backbone, but Mitchell truly was rude more often than not.

That was something that had been a trait of his father's, and Tosha couldn't believe she hadn't seen it until they were married. Of course, they hadn't been dating long until she got pregnant with Mitchell, and they decided to get married to make it official.

Of course, that didn't even last two years. Two years and two kids.

"Mitchell, try to be nice," she said. "Bailey. You're fine. Whether or not he likes the girls' restroom has nothing to do with you."

She felt like she mediated like this constantly between the two of them. That was mostly through guilt. Because if it hadn't been for her poor decisions, they would have a stable home, instead of being shifted from home to home, with her sometimes having a job and sometimes she got child support and sometimes not. Right now, she had no idea where their dad was and no idea if he was working or not. She hadn't seen any money for several months.

She got out and started on the job of getting the children out. To her surprise, Tobias got out on his side and then opened the door and started to get River out of her car seat.

In her experience, the man she was with did not help with the children. Ever. And particularly with car seats.

She was starting to get the idea that Tobias was a little different.

She continued to get that idea as they walked toward the building, her carrying Phoenix in his car seat and holding on to Gemmy's hand.

Tobias had River in his arms, and Mitchell hung close to him as well.

Bailey was the only one who didn't have someone.

It made her feel bad for her daughter, who so often got pushed aside by the younger ones who demanded attention. Maybe that was why Bailey had her feelings hurt so often and easily. She felt like she wasn't being seen by her mother.

As they walked toward the building, a lone man walked toward them. Tosha, because of the way she'd been living the last few years, was used to being on alert, and she didn't like the way that man looked at her children, especially Bailey.

Before she could move, Tobias had switched River from one arm to the other and moved closer to Bailey, putting a hand on her shoulder, right by her neck.

He didn't pull her toward him, but from his position, it was obvious that he was showing that man that the children and family were his, and he would protect them.

At least that was what Tosha read into his actions. The man's eyes skittered away, and he moved over some on the sidewalk so that they passed with a good distance between them.

Tosha didn't say anything, but she tucked that thought away. She never really had anyone who had helped her out like that with the children. It was usually up to her to be the protector.

Not that the man posed any real sense of danger, it just made her feel good to know that Tobias would have her back and would go to bat for her.

And the children. Most of all, for the children.

She swallowed. She was not going to develop feelings for this man. He'd been obvious about how he felt about her, barely able to stand her, metaphorically holding his nose while he helped her. Doing her grandma a favor or something. She wasn't sure. She thought about that as she helped the children go to the bathroom, and then she walked out to where Mitchell and Tobias stood, in front of the map. Tobias was pointing at something, and Mitchell was talking.

She wanted to stop and just look at the scene. Mitchell actually seemed interested in something? Other than getting into trouble?

It seemed too good to be true, but yet, there it was. Tobias was talking to the boy like he meant something and was not treating him like an irritating gnat that needed to be brushed away.

"I saw a table over there. If you don't mind, I'll get Phoenix's diaper out and change him and feed him, and the kids can run around right there." There were some trees, and it was all open, but it was not too close to the road where the cars would be coming in and out.

"All right. You lead the way." Tobias glanced up, looked around, his eyes going to each of the children, before he went back and put his hand on Mitchell's shoulder.

Mitchell straightened under his hand, almost as though he were proud to be beside Tobias.

Lord, no. Please don't let Mitchell fall in love with this man and idolize him, only to have one more person walk out of his life.

She needed to ask this man exactly what his intentions were, because she was not going to allow her children to be hurt by him in any way.

Chapter Six

Tobias watched the kids play as Tosha finished changing the baby. He felt like he had a hundred things to say to her, even more, but he wasn't sure where to start.

He sat down on the top of the picnic table, putting his feet on the seat and resting his forearms on his knees.

He was able to see better from up here, and while Tosha had given the kids clear directions about where their boundaries were while they were playing, Tobias wasn't completely sure Mitchell would obey. After all, if the kid would get in a car and start driving down the street, he certainly wasn't going to worry about any kind of imaginary boundaries his mom set in the rest area. But from here, Tobias could make sure that no one was approaching the children to do any harm to them. Or to take them. They were under his protection, and Tobias was not going to allow anything to happen to them on his watch.

Plus, it was funny the way spending a few hours with kids could make a man want to make sure nothing terrible ever happened to them.

"You said you wanted to talk to me when the children were gone?" Tosha asked as she pulled the pants up on the baby and sat down on the seat, propping one ankle up on her leg and putting the bottle in the baby's mouth. She moved slowly, almost as though she didn't even realize what she was doing, and her eyes were trained on his face, questions in them, before they looked back to check on her children.

She was very alert and aware too, and he appreciated that. Rest areas had a bad reputation, although he had never seen anything bad happening in any that he had ever stopped at. That didn't mean that he was going to let down his guard.

"I wanted to talk about eating. I didn't know if you wanted to stop and get fast food, or if you wanted to take the kids and sit down somewhere? Are you picky about what they get? I assume they're going to be hungry."

"I packed some snacks. And I have more in my bag, just crackers and bottles of water and that type of thing in the bag at my feet. So, we probably don't actually need to stop for food if you don't want to."

"Won't it be better for them if we do?"

"Yes. But I don't want to inconvenience you."

"Children are an inconvenience. That's just what they are. But you do it because...because it's right." He almost said "because you love them." That would be the right reason, wouldn't it? But if he couldn't do it out of love, he could do it out of duty.

"Yes. Although, I love my children and want what's best for them, so that's probably my motivation." Her words came out casual, not like she was trying to teach him a lesson, which she obviously wasn't. No one expected him to love her children. Least of all her. She'd been very clear that she was giving him the cold shoulder. Not that he felt like he was giving any kind of signals that he was interested in a relationship, but maybe he was. After all, he had planned to ask her to marry him. And maybe he was giving out signals he didn't realize he was.

"Then you're a good mother," he said.

She snorted. But she didn't say anything, and he didn't follow through with that. Why would she snort derisively when he said she was a good mother? But maybe he knew the answer to that question. And maybe she was trying to change. It seemed like she was, although it was hard. After all, it took a person of character and integrity to look at their life and say that they weren't doing everything right, and maybe they should make some changes. Most people would say that they're doing okay and not be interested in having any kind of guidance from someone else.

"Is that all you wanted to talk to me about?" she asked, and he got the feeling that she wanted to get up and run away.

"For now." He had a lot of other things to talk to her about, but this hardly seemed like the time. Could he propose to her while they sat at a picnic table at a rest area? He wasn't intending to be romantic, that really wasn't in his DNA, except... Maybe she needed that. Maybe if he intended to make her his wife, he owed that to her. No matter what his motives were for getting married. He thought again about the letter, about the clear instructions that he felt like he had received from the board. About the money, about how it could change everything. But... did he want things to change? He was happy and content with his life.

At least he used to be.

But he would never be happy and content if he wasn't in the center of God's will.

"All right. If you're done, I have a few things I want to talk about with you." She sounded defensive, almost like she was challenging him.

"All right," he said, deliberately making his voice easy, nonthreatening. His hands were loose between his knees. His posture as nonthreatening as possible.

"What are your intentions?" she asked, almost as though she were grilling him about him wanting to marry her daughter.

"My intentions?" His brows furrowed, and he gave her a questioning look before looking back at the children. There was a couple walking close by, but they were holding hands and talking, and he didn't think they were a threat. There was a single man over at the far picnic table, who he'd been keeping an eye on. There were also two older ladies and another older couple walking a dog.

No one seemed to be interested in the kids, but that didn't mean that he was going to take his eyes off them.

"Why are you doing this?"

"Helping you?" he asked, trying to get a read on her face, but she just looked confused and maybe even a little angry.

"Yeah. Coming to my house, picking us up, hiring movers, stopping when I ask you to, being kind to my children, and even acting a little defensive about them. Even now, you're watching them like a hawk, and if I'm not mistaken, you know exactly what's going on in the perimeter, and you're keeping your eye on that single man over there at the picnic table."

"As well as that couple right there, and I'm not real sure about that group of men right there." He nodded over the side. A group of men that had been talking the whole time they'd been standing there. He didn't think that they had any nefarious intentions either, but he wasn't sure. "And there's those two women right there, middle-aged, and not shabby, but not super well-dressed either. I honestly am not sure whether most children get abducted by women or men, but I'm keeping my eye on both genders."

"Why? Why are you doing this for me? For my kids?"

"I've worked with your grandma for a while now. She's a nice lady. She's worried about you. I knew you needed help, from talking to her. Is it so unusual that someone might come and help someone just for the sake of helping them?"

"Yeah. It is."

"Well, I guess that's what Christians are supposed to do." He didn't want to blame it on being a Christian. Although, he would have helped her gram and had, for no pay. In fact, he sunk a lot of his own money into Gram's house, not that her gram knew about it. She thought she was paying for everything, and he just didn't bother to tell her that what she was paying for was barely a drop in the bucket. There was no need to do that. Maybe the woman suspected it.

"So you're a Christian." The statement was said flatly. Her eyes turned away.

"Aren't you?"

"I used to believe. I used to believe in Santa Claus too."

"I bet you still believe. Bet if you thought about it and reasoned it out, your logic would make you more inclined to believe than not."

"I'm sorry. But I just don't believe that."

"We can talk about it if you want to," he said, figuring that she probably didn't want to. And he wasn't sure he did. What was the point in having a long, drawn-out conversation? Although he couldn't imagine marrying someone who wasn't going to go to church with him.

Would that be Tosha? Would he end up in church by himself while his family stayed home?

Lord, I don't want to go to church by myself. If I'm going to be married, I want my wife beside me.

Better than that, he wanted her beside him, tucked up close, smiling up at him, and laughing, enjoying the time that they worshiped the Lord together, while they made memories at home that would make them smile and share the secret glances that married couples had.

He hadn't known he wanted those things.

"Not today. I want to know what your deal is. Why are you doing this? And don't give me some song and dance about it being because you're Christian."

"I do a lot of things because I'm a Christian. That actually guides pretty much everything I do. Including sitting here talking to you." He wasn't going to lie about that. Being a Christian had changed his life. He would be a completely different person if he didn't know Jesus.

"So that's why you're doing this?" She let the question hang there in the air while the baby nursed happily on the bottle. Shouts from the kids floated over to them as the wind blew gently, and the sound of motors on the interstate was ever present.

Thankfully it was a sunny, mostly warm day, with blue skies and perfect weather.

Any other time, he might be sitting here, truly interested in developing a relationship with the woman beside him. Although, he was, wasn't he? He did want to have a relationship with his wife. But he didn't figure it would ever include secret smiles and shared memories.

Maybe it would. Maybe he wasn't giving God enough credit. God could certainly do anything, including making his arranged marriage into a love match. Or maybe just making the woman that he was going to propose marriage to actually want to love him. Since he believed love was a choice. And he was going to choose it, although what he thought love was and what she did were probably two different things.

"I suppose you're right. I do have some ulterior motives." She seemed to guess that, and he didn't see any point beating around the bush about it.

"I knew you did. But you seemed to indicate that it wasn't sex. Am I wrong?"

She was blunt. He'd give her that.

"I made a vow that I wouldn't have sex with anyone I wasn't married to." He could be just as blunt.

She snorted again. "It sucks to be a Christian." She laughed.

"I don't have five kids with dads scattered everywhere."

"I would hope not. Since you're a man." But there wasn't nearly as much laughter in her voice that time. He had hit a nerve, and he wished he could take those words back. He didn't want to fight and definitely didn't want to put her down. He understood how bad choices could ruin a person's life. Thankfully, his parents had guided him in the right way, and he'd listened. He'd seen some kids with great parents who'd made terrible decisions and spent the rest of their lives regretting them.

"You're right." He didn't have a problem telling someone they were right when they were. It seemed that if a fight was going to happen, it would be because people refused to concede even the smallest point to the person they were talking to.

"You're right too. You're absolutely right. I'm sorry I kind of made fun of you."

"You're not the first person." That was the truth. He didn't want to go there, because he tried not to think about that. But there were people who made fun of him for the different stands he took because he was a Christian. There were things he didn't seek after, things he didn't listen to, things he didn't do. All of them had gotten him made fun of and teased throughout school and even as an adult. It was funny that people made fun of another person because they didn't do bad things. What was wrong with that?

"All right. I'm sorry. I actually admire that. And if I'd been smart, I would have done the same thing."

He felt like this was the real her, a little bit vulnerable but sincere. Someone who wished that she would have waited for the right person.

"You know, we can look back at our lives and wish that we would have made different decisions. I certainly have at times. But God uses our mistakes to shape us and grow us. He also uses them to move us where He wants us to be. Maybe you did all of those things and had your five children so that you could meet me."

That seemed kind of arrogant, and she gave another derisive snort.

"I don't mean that in an arrogant way. But if it hadn't been for those choices and your children and those men that have come and gone, I wouldn't be here right now, right?"

"All right. I see what you're saying. I thought you were saying that the end goal of my life was for God to make me meet you, and I do think that you were rather full of yourself to think that God would orchestrate all of this in my life just for the end goal of meeting Tobias Clybourn."

"No. Tobias Clybourn isn't anybody. Not without Jesus."

Chapter Seven

Tosha stared at the man beside her. He just admitted that he wasn't anything without Jesus. And yet, he looked so respectable, so honest, so upright. To the point where she felt a little embarrassed to be with him. Although, proud too. Could she be embarrassed and proud at the same time?

She knew how the people that she normally hung out with would make fun of him. They would tease him and call him all kinds of stupid names. They would try to get him to be like them. And yet, they weren't happy. But Tobias seemed confident and calm and in control. Like nothing was going to shake him. Very much unlike any of the other men she knew.

She had been a Christian when she was younger. She remembered asking Jesus to save her, but it seemed like Christians were boring. Stuck in the mud. People who had more things they didn't do than things that they did. And who wanted to be the person who didn't get drunk and didn't do drugs and didn't have sex and didn't sneak out and have fun?

And yet, where had that gotten her? Here, with a whole big pile of regrets. And like Tobias had hinted at, she wished she could go back and make different choices. And like she admitted, she wished she could make the same choice he had, to resist the allure of the world and to say that she wasn't going to have sex with anyone she wasn't married to.

That would have made most of the boys that she had been with, all the boys, actually, go running from her. Because they weren't interested in her if there wasn't sex involved.

"So I'm supposed to believe that the reason that you're doing this is because you are Christian and you wanted to?"

"I just told you I have ulterior motives."

"So what are your ulterior motives?" she asked, figuring that sex was probably the furthest thing from his mind.

"You don't think you have anything that I could want?" he asked easily.

"Do I?"

"You have experience that I don't have."

"You don't want my experience."

"Says who?" he asked, and that made her turn her attention completely away from her children and onto him. What in the world could he mean?

"You. You are a Christian, you said. You don't do the things I did. Why would you be interested in my experience?"

"Maybe I found the girl I want, and I don't know how to kiss. Maybe I need kissing lessons."

She couldn't help it. Her jaw hung open as she looked at this man, solid and strong beside her, deep blue eyes, strong nose, granite jaw, broad shoulders. He looked like he worked for a living and was capable of doing pretty much anything. And yet, he was casually telling her that he wanted kissing lessons?

"I don't believe that for one second." She dismissed him, tossed her head, and looked back at her children. The group of men had left, but the single man was still sitting at the table. He did have his phone out and seemed to be texting on it, but every once in a while, he would look up. The two ladies Tobias had pointed out were still around as well.

"I'm not asking for payment. But if you'd like to pay me, I'll take some kissing lessons."

Her throat had gone dry, and she did not look at him but stared unseeing in the direction of her children.

There was something about his words that made some kind of electricity run from the top of her head the whole way to her feet and back, seeming to light up her heart in a really weird but pleasurable way.

She would not mind giving that man kissing lessons.

But no. She'd sworn off men.

"I'm sorry. You're right, I probably could give you kissing lessons," she said, not wanting him to think that she was trying to be some kind of pure maiden that she absolutely was not. "But I made a decision when the last man left, when I was pregnant with Phoenix, that I would not be sucked in by men anymore. Not for anything. I am done with men."

She probably could go on and on and turn it into a rant about how men were no good, had done nothing but bad in her life, had treated her terribly, and had never stuck around or been around when she needed them.

But she didn't need to sound as bitter and angry as she felt at times. And on such a beautiful day, she really didn't want to think about that at all. What she wanted to think about was kissing lessons. But only with Tobias.

"I think that's a good thing. I think one man is enough, and that's the man you spend the rest of your life."

"Good luck finding someone like that. I have yet to find a man who actually wanted to settle down with one woman. I can't tell you the number of times I've been cheated on."

"I can tell you the number of women I've cheated on. It's a big fat zero. And I can tell you the number of women that I'll ever cheat on, and it's the same."

It might have sounded arrogant coming from anyone else, but from Tobias, it sounded like flat facts.

"All right then. Good for you. Good for me too."

"It's not good for you to be alone. There should be someone with whom you spend the rest of your life with."

"Well, I seem to attract the kind of men who are here and then gone, and sometimes I don't even know what prompted the gone. I just know I'm told to get my stuff and leave."

That did sound bitter, and she couldn't help it. She didn't really want to help it. She wanted to talk about something, anything else. Why in the world was this man talking to her about this anyway?

"You're gonna drop me off at my grandma's house, and then you're leaving, and I'll never see you again."

"Sweet Water's a small town. I'm sure we'll run into each other."

He seemed like he might be hiding something, and she wanted to look at him, as though she could figure out what it was, but she didn't want to make eye contact. She needed to resist it, because the idea of kissing lessons was buzzing around in her head, and she really wanted to take him up on that offer. After all, there would be no strings attached. He wouldn't be expecting anything more than kissing, because he told her himself that he wasn't having sex with anyone he wasn't married to, and he certainly wasn't going to be married to her. So she didn't have to worry about him wanting more.

They'd just be kissing, which was fun, pleasurable, and with no strings attached, she could do it without guilt.

Did she really want to add one more man to the list of men that she kissed?

She had vowed no one. Ever again.

"I'm pretty good at avoiding people." She finally managed to respond to his comment.

"I guess we'll see how good you are," he said simply.

Phoenix finished his bottle and pushed away from her, trying to sit up, wanting to see what was going on around him.

"You think he's ready to go?"

"I think so. We probably all are. I do really appreciate you allowing the children to have time to run around and burn off some energy. Maybe, if we're lucky, at least two or three of them will fall asleep, and we'll have another pretty happy four hours."

"It won't matter if they're in the back screaming at the top of their lungs, it's not going to bother me."

"Crying kids bother men. And that's just a fact of life." She hadn't met anyone who didn't care whether or not the kid was crying. She did meet a few that were willing to turn the TV set up so loud they couldn't hear them, but most of them would yell at her like it was her responsibility to get them to stop, no matter whether their name was on the birth certificate or not. Thankfully she only had two kids who actually had a father listed on the birth certificate, and that was Mitchell and Bailey. And that was before she had gotten wise to the ways of men and had realized that it was far easier to get full custody of her children if she was the only one who was listed.

As they worked to gather the kids up and put them back in the car, Tobias still just using his body language to let the people around them know that this was his family and his responsibility, and he was watching out for these kids, she thought about what he had said. That he did have ulterior motives. And somehow, she didn't think that the kissing lessons were actually what he meant.

Chapter Eight

Tobias walked out of the hotel lobby, two room keys in his hand. He and Tosha hadn't talked a whole lot over the last four hours, but they had decided that they would stop and get a hotel for the evening.

Tosha hadn't seemed overly excited about it, and he figured it was because she was afraid he was going to make her share a room. He wasn't sure. But whatever it was, she didn't have to worry about that. He hadn't put her mind at rest, because he wasn't sure that was her issue. Still, he fingered the keys, shoving them in his back pocket and walking to the SUV where Tosha waited with the children.

He wasn't sure why he had told her that he had ulterior motives, other than he didn't want to lie to her. He didn't want to ever lie to anyone, but most especially not to Tosha. Regardless of whether she would marry him or not, he knew she was the woman that God had clearly told him he was to marry. So, if Tosha wouldn't have him, he wouldn't get married. He'd thought that once before in his life too, so he amended it to say that unless God showed him someone else.

What was it about him that seemed to make women not want him?

That wasn't a fair question. It wasn't like he was going after women, because he really wasn't. He was just biding his time, keeping an eye out, but not seeing anyone interesting, or interested, come along.

Really, he spent the last four hours castigating himself because he'd talked about kissing lessons with Tosha. If he was being honest, part of him was rather intimidated by the fact that she was obviously experienced in areas that he absolutely was not. Maybe that was why it was so easy for him to say that he had made a decision not to have sex with anyone before he was married. He wanted her to know what he was. A person couldn't tell by looking at someone, although he did give off certain vibes, of that he was sure.

She knew a lot of things he didn't, and for him to say it wasn't intimidating for him would be a lie. After all, he wanted to do what God wanted him to do, but he also wanted to be a good husband. Someone his wife could look at with longing on her face.

He snorted. It was hard to picture Tosha looking at him with any kind of softness.

Although she wasn't a hard woman, considering what she had been through. Not hard in any area except when she said that she was not going to allow another man into her life. She had been firm about that.

And rightfully so. He could totally understand it and couldn't blame her, except... He wanted her to let him in. Just him. No one else.

From what she said, she blamed the men who walked out on her. He hoped that was true, but he really had no assurance that she would stay, and part of him didn't expect her to. After all, he was the one with the mandate from the Lord, not her.

He reached the car, opening up the door and sticking his head in. "I've got our rooms, and—"

"Rooms?" Tosha interrupted him before he could finish.

"Yes. Two."

He wasn't sure if that was relief on her face or disappointment. It couldn't have been disappointment. He shook his head at himself, but waited until she responded with a nod to his statement, and then continued. "And the clerk said that this is the best place to park. We'll go in through those doors I just came out of."

"All right. We only want to carry changes of clothes for the kids and their jammies. I have those packed right on top of the bags that we put in the back. There should be four, and I have a baby bag for Phoenix we can carry in."

"What about you?" he asked.

She lifted her brows for a moment and blinked, as though she wasn't used to anyone asking about her. "I have some things too. I... I can grab those as well."

He had brought a change of clothes, but he didn't own jammies.

"I assumed that Mitchell would stay with me. There are two queen beds on my side, and I asked for adjoining rooms. But if you don't want that, it's up to you."

"That'll be fine. Actually, that would be wonderful. If he stays in your room, there will be plenty of space for the rest of us. Gemmy can sleep with me, and River can share with Bailey, and Phoenix... We can put him in the pack and play if you don't mind carrying it in? Or if you don't mind watching the kids while I go back out and get it."

"I'll carry it in," he said, and maybe there was a little bit of annoyance in his voice. They had just spent the entire day together, and he hadn't shied away from helping with the children. It was a little bit annoying that she still wasn't sure that he would actually help her or not.

But it was wrong of him to get annoyed, because of course she didn't know. She was around people who didn't care about her and weren't interested in helping. If that's all she'd known, she would expect him to fit in that box. It was up to him to show her that he didn't.

"You will?" she asked, and then she blinked. "Thank you. I appreciate that. That would be a huge help."

"I'll help you get the kids in first, and then I'll come back out for that, and I have a change of clothes in an overnight bag here too."

"Of course. You can carry that in first."

"I'll help you with the children. Maybe Mitchell will come back out with me." He looked at the boy who seemed to pop out his chest and lift his head as he realized that he'd been singled out to go back out with the strange man who had suddenly jumped into their lives today.

It seemed like Mitchell liked him okay, and Tobias figured that if it were possible, he would use that to his advantage. Not that he wanted to manipulate the child, exactly, but the kid needed to be taken in hand if he wasn't going to continue down the path that he had obviously been going down, and it would make it a lot easier if Mitchell liked and respected Tobias. It might not be necessary to use punishment, but rather encouragement to get the kid to do what he was supposed to do.

He hadn't realized what a parade they would make as the two of them and the five kids walked into the hotel. They turned heads at every step. Not that the hotel was busy, because it wasn't, with just five or six people in the lobby area, and they met one on their way to the elevator. They all gave them amazed looks, although there were a couple of derisive looks, and he could almost hear someone saying that they were contributing to the overpopulation of the world.

He supposed people were entitled to their opinion, but when their opinion caused them to look down on someone else who held a different opinion, it was annoying. But he was not on a crusade to change anyone's mind, no one other than Tosha.

And this was what she endured all the time.

He was glad he didn't mind being conspicuous, because they certainly were as they got off the elevator and went down the hall, the children being quieter than he would have expected. He held River, who seemed to have taken a shine to him, in one of his arms, while he carried Phoenix in his car seat in the other. Tosha had been surprised when he had offered to take him and had let him go willingly as she herded all the children with their bags.

"These are the two rooms," he said as they reached rooms 321 and 323.

"Can I open it?" Bailey said eagerly, looking up at him with shining eyes.

"I'll do it," Mitchell said in a tone that wasn't quite kind.

"Bailey's going to be in this room. Let her open her door, and you can open ours, but you need to be nice about it," Tobias said, and there was no anger or unkindness in his voice. He made sure to keep his tone modulated and matter-of-fact.

Mitchell, to his surprise, did not get a belligerent look on his face but rather jerked his head and stepped back so Bailey could get her card.

"Thank you," Bailey said, giving him a shy smile.

It seemed to take her forever to get the key out of the package, and Mitchell was obviously chomping at the bit to take it from her and do it himself.

Tosha looked exhausted as she held Gemmy and two bags along with the baby bag over her shoulder.

He should have told her he would go back down for everything so that she could go in and sit down, although it was far from her being able to rest. She would have to get all the kids in, get them cleaned up if she was going to give them baths or anything, and she had leftovers from when they stopped at a fast-food place for lunch to feed them.

He had wanted to go out for supper, but she had insisted that they would just get a couple of extra sandwiches and that would be fine.

He wasn't sure whether she was trying to save money, or whether she didn't want to deal with the kids in a restaurant after a long day of driving. He would have done fast food again. But they didn't talk about it, and he just did what she wanted.

After they opened their door, he held it while Tosha and the kids walked in and Mitchell opened theirs.

He allowed the door to close behind them, meeting Tosha's eyes. She indicated the adjoining door and walked over. He assumed she was going to open it.

"Do I get to choose my bed?" Mitchell asked as he easily unlocked the door from their side and opened it.

"You sure can, unless your mom has a preference. And then we'll do what she wants, because you honor your mother and obey her."

He figured that kids just needed a lot of repetition, so he was going to push that home to Mitchell as often as he could. He had his doubts about whether or not it would stick, but it wasn't his job to make it stick. It was his job to teach it, to model it, to use every means possible to instruct this young boy who would someday be a man and hopefully live for Jesus.

Having the children separated into two separate rooms seemed to make it so that it wasn't quite as chaotic on the other side. Or maybe he was just getting used to the chaos as Gemmy ran around, being chased by River, and Bailey's mouth was going a mile a minute about the view outside and about wanting to take a bath and having the water as deep as she wanted it and asking if she could jump on the bed.

Tosha looked exhausted, and he wished there was something he could do to give her a break. But he supposed that was what having children was, chaos, constant work, and never getting a break.

He felt tired himself, but he said to her as she turned and smiled at the open door, "I'll go back down and get the pack and play. Is there anything else you need?"

"I forgot to bring the food out. And there was water at my feet."

"I can bring that in, although I can check the lobby and see if we can get some cold water. I would prefer that anyway. Would you like some coffee?"

"I would love some, but I better not have any, or I'll be lying in bed staring at the ceiling at two o'clock in the morning, and then I'll be grumpy tomorrow."

"And if Mom gets grumpy, watch out," Mitchell said, surprising Tobias, who hadn't realized that the kid was listening to the conversation. He should have known he would be. At that age, the kids didn't want to miss anything.

He could remember listening to his parents talk and not wanting to miss a word. It seemed like everything they said was so much more interesting than anything else that was going on. Although, if he had a choice between listening and playing, he would always choose playing.

He'd have to remember that with the young children. Although, he didn't think they would have a problem finding things to play with at the farm. Especially after living in the city as they had.

"I'll be back." He looked at Mitchell. "Would you like to come with me?"

The kid nodded his head eagerly, and Tobias pointed at the key card.

"You want to take it? That way, we'll be able to let ourselves in and won't be at the mercy of your mom and sisters."

"Yeah. I think I will."

"Put it in your pocket so you don't lose it."

The kid obeyed immediately, and Tobias had a hard time reconciling this child, who did everything he asked him to, with the kid who had gotten in his car and driven it down the road.

Maybe he really just needed a man in his life, or some attention, or both.

Whatever it was, he had an idea that maybe God had brought him into this family for a reason.

<h1 style="text-align:center">Chapter Nine</h1>

After Tobias had set up the pack and play, he asked if she would be able to talk to him when she had all the kids down for the night.

Despite their excessive energy from sitting in the car all day, they were all tired too, and it was less than two hours later that she had given them all baths, gotten their clean jammies on, fed them the leftovers from lunch, and had them in bed.

The doors between the two rooms weren't shut tight, but she still knocked before she pushed his open.

"You can come on in. Mitchell fell asleep an hour ago, right after his shower." Tobias's voice was low.

"Should we go out to the hall to talk?" she asked.

"That might be a good idea, if you're okay with it?"

"I think mine are asleep, and we'll have less chance of waking them up if we head out for a few minutes."

"We're not to be gone long, and we can stand right outside the door."

She nodded, and they didn't say anything more while he picked up his key and quietly opened the door without making any noise at all.

She had no idea how he did it. He could be more quiet than she, despite the fact that she assumed she had a lot more practice, at least in trying not to wake up kids.

He was in his bare feet, wearing a T-shirt and jeans, looking a lot more casual than he had in his button-down all day. His hair was wet from the shower, although he hadn't shaved.

She liked the short beard. It took her a moment to remember that she wasn't supposed to be looking and rip her eyes away. It was so tempting to get into a familiar routine with him. He made it easy. Taking care of the children, helping without harassing, and being more considerate than anyone she'd ever met.

"I didn't really have anything to talk about, other than wanting to know what time you wanted to leave in the morning. I think we have another eight hours of driving, and I'm not in a huge rush to get home, but you'll know what's best for the kids."

"They're going to be hungry."

"There's an all-you-can-eat breakfast downstairs from six to nine. Can we feed them there?"

"Yeah. They'll probably be up at six, too."

"All right. Would you like to text me when they're up, and we can chat like that?"

She hadn't even considered giving him her phone number. That would have made this a lot easier and unnecessary. They could have just texted instead of standing out in the hall whispering to each other. But maybe part of her didn't want to give him her number because she wanted to be able to stand out in the hall with him. Wanted to see him, wanted to be around him.

The more time she spent with Tobias, the more curious she was about him. What did he do for a living? How could he have the time to come out and move a woman and her five children to North Dakota? Where did he live? He said Sweet Water was a small town and they would see each other around. Did that mean he lived there? What did he do? What was his life like?

He talked about kissing lessons, although the more she thought about that, the more she thought he was teasing her and she just hadn't realized it because she didn't expect him to have a sense of humor. But he obviously wasn't married. He said he'd been waiting for the right one. Or at least he hadn't been intimate with anyone, so she assumed that meant he was waiting. So much of what she knew about him were assumptions that she'd made based on what he had said.

She'd like to find out whether those assumptions were true or not.

Tonight wasn't the night.

"I'll give you my number," she said, waiting for him to pull his phone out of his pocket so he could type it in.

"If I send you a text, I don't want to wake the children up."

"It's okay. I always have my phone on silent. A mom learns these things," she said. She really did feel comfortable with him. He...seemed to be easygoing but commanding at the same time. She'd never quite seen that combination in a man before, and she had to admit it was extremely appealing. But more than that, he had a sense about him that he was going to do right no matter what.

It was like he carried his character on his sleeve, rather than his heart.

She found it very appealing, especially after the kind of men she seemed to have been attracted to when she was young and dumb. Maybe this was just a sign that she was growing up, and she wasn't really falling for this man who was silent and strong yet tender and sweet and so adorable when he held her little girl.

"I just want to thank you for everything today. I know I was a little prickly at times, and I'm sorry about that. I guess I just don't trust people very easily."

"I can totally understand why you wouldn't." There was a short pause. "I assume we're leaving the doors open between the rooms."

It took her a moment to understand what he was saying. "I never thought that you would do anything like that with Mitchell."

"I just wanted you to know that the doors are open, and you can check any time. He's in the bed by the window. His choice."

She smiled. Mitchell and Tobias seemed to have hit it off. Mitchell especially seemed to be totally infatuated with Tobias and had dogged his footsteps as much as Tobias would allow him, which was a lot. She had never had another man around who had been as patient with Mitchell as what Tobias was.

"I suppose I should thank you for that as well."

"Leaving the doors open?" he said, sounding puzzled, of course.

"For what you do with Mitchell. After the way you met him, I could understand if you had a chip on your shoulder against him or felt like he needed to be put in his place."

"I just assumed he has had some life experiences that have shaped him in ways that I probably couldn't imagine and wouldn't understand."

"That's pretty big of you. Sometimes when you haven't been in someone's shoes, you don't realize how different those shoes are from your own."

"Sometimes," he said, nodding. He stuck one hand in his pocket and hooked another hand around his neck, almost as though he were uncomfortable in some way.

Maybe he wasn't used to standing out in the hallway of a hotel at night, whispering to some woman he barely knew.

"I'll let you get to bed. You're probably tired."

"I can see that you are. If there's something I can do to help you, you can let me know. You know that, right?"

She supposed deep down, she really did know that. But maybe there was a part of her that didn't want to admit it. Maybe there was a part of her that still resented him in some way, because he'd made better decisions, smarter decisions than she had, and he'd gotten into a place in his life where she wished she was, but she couldn't see any way there. Like there was a chasm between the two of them that could never be crossed. It reminded her of that story in the Bible that she heard when she was still going to church. The one about the rich man talking to Abraham, and there being an uncrossable chasm between them.

"Thank you. I appreciate it," she finally said.

He waited for just a moment, and then without saying anything, he tapped his card on the door and opened it, holding it so she could go through.

When's the last time she had a man who had manners and acted like a gentleman and treated her like a lady?

It was a rhetorical question, because the answer was never. She never had anyone who had been as kind to her as Tobias had been just today. Even when she was first dating anyone, they had never treated her this well.

"Good night," she said as she slipped into his room and then walked between the adjoining doors.

She still needed to take a shower, but she was looking forward to getting into bed. Every muscle in her body ached; it had been a hard day. But it would have been a lot harder without Tobias. She'd have been driving and trying to handle all of the children, then trying to keep them together at the rest area and run herd on them while she fed Phoenix. She wouldn't have wanted to stay long, because she would have been afraid that she couldn't keep an eye on all five of them like she needed to.

Regardless, she appreciated what he had done and wondered if there was anything that she could do to pay him back. Had he been serious about his kissing lessons?

Chapter Ten

The drive the next day was a little harder. Tobias wasn't sure why. Whether it was because he was impatient to be home, or whether the kids were just sick of riding, he wasn't sure. Regardless, they were antsy, and they ended up stopping three times, twice at rest areas and once at another fast-food restaurant. Tosha had begged him not to go in and sit down with the kids. She said they were usually pretty well behaved, but when they had been cooped up in a car for days on end and everyone's tempers were short and they were all eager to get away from each other, a restaurant meal would be a disaster.

He didn't care. For him, food was food. And he just ate what was put in front of him. He supposed it had to do with growing up with eleven siblings. And come to think of it, he and Tosha hadn't talked about his family at all. She had no idea he had eleven siblings, and she also had no idea that he was living with her grandmother. There were a lot of things she had no idea about.

He probably ought to see if he could get her to agree to marry him before she found out some of the things she didn't know. She might be angry, and then he'd have a harder time than he would if she had already agreed. Surely she wouldn't go back on her word.

Of course she would. People did. New information came along, and people changed. It was hard to find someone who actually did what they said they were going to do.

He was still thinking about that as they drove down the streets of Sweet Water.

"This is the town, Sweet Water. The closest one to your gram's."

"It's really small," she said, looking around at the diner and the hardware store, and the new grocery store that had opened a few years ago.

"It's growing. But I hope it doesn't grow too much. It's perfect the way it is."

She didn't say anything, and they were soon on the other side of town, passing the auction barn, and out on the open country again. He turned north and drove for a couple of miles before he pointed to a lane off to the left.

"That's where my family lives."

"Your family?" she said, ignoring the kids in the back as River squabbled with Gemmy over something that Tobias at least couldn't understand. Gemmy could talk, but her words were a little bit difficult to make out, unless a person listened closely. Tobias wasn't quite sure how Tosha could do it.

"Yeah. My siblings."

"You have siblings. How many?"

"Eleven." He waited for the explosion of disbelief. He was used to it by now. It had happened all his life any time anyone had asked that question.

"Oh my goodness. Eleven siblings? No wonder you're so weird."

He'd heard that before. And a host of other things. "Yeah. eleven. I'm number four."

"Wow, stuck in the middle. Of course, there's a lot of you stuck in the middle if there are twelve of you altogether."

"Yeah. Although my parents were amazing. They did a great job."

"Were?"

"Yeah. They passed away in a car accident a dozen or so years ago. My siblings and I moved here from Wyoming."

"I see. So you didn't grow up in Sweet Water?"

"No."

"Wait a minute. You didn't say you lived with them."

"I don't."

"Do all your siblings live on the ranch together?"

"They do."

"Except for you?"

"I have two younger siblings who are in college right now. But when they come home, Sweet Water is home. One of my sisters is thinking about moving back to Wyoming too."

That seemed to distract her enough that she didn't follow up with her questioning to ask where he actually lived, and just in case she was thinking about it, he pointed off in the distance. "Your gram lives right over that hill. This is her land here on the right."

"Wow. This is Gram's?"

"It is."

"It's so much that you can't even see the house. I know she said she owned a thousand acres, but it sounded, I don't know, big but not so big that...there's nothing else close by." She looked around, seeming to be uncomfortable that there were no other houses in the area.

"You get used to it. Everyone in town feels like your neighbor. And anyone who's around will give you a hand. That's just the way we are out here. Because you're right, it can be kind of vast and empty. And you feel like you're all alone if you don't know that you have that human connection."

"You lived here long enough to figure that out?"

"It was like that in Wyoming too. A little different, but very similar. The people here appear hearty, maybe not heartier, but just tough. Because it's a tough climate. You have to be tough."

"Maybe I'm not tough enough to live in North Dakota," Tosha said, and while her words were light, her face held concern.

"Oh, you're tough enough. Anyone who can have five children and take care of them all on a trip from Sioux City to Sweet Water is tough enough to live in Sweet Water."

She glanced at him, and there was surprise in her eyes, like it was surprising for her to know that he had been watching her.

Maybe just as surprising as him asking for kissing lessons. That was such a stupid idea. He didn't know why the words had come out of his mouth other than she intimidated him, and because if she agreed to his proposal, he probably would be kissing her at some point, and she'd obviously been kissed a lot.

"I guess I'll take your word for it." She took a deep breath as though she was steadying herself and then looked out the window. "I don't know about you, but I'm ready to get out of the car for a while."

"There's plenty of space to run around at your gram's." He grinned. "For you and the kids."

"You're smiling. Either you like the idea of getting out of the car and not having to spend all this time with me again, or—"

"Or I'm just as eager to get out of this thing as everyone else is."

That was entirely true. To his surprise, he was a little bit sad Tosha wasn't going to be forced to spend time with him. He had grown to enjoy her company. Which, he had to admit, surprised him. He wasn't expecting to like her. But he realized, as he put his signal on and turned into her gram's lane, he did. A lot.

Chapter Eleven

osha could remember one time, vaguely, when she had been a little girl that she had visited her gram. Nothing looked familiar though. Maybe it was because the porch seemed to be new, or because the house seemed to be freshly painted. But even the shape seemed wrong somehow.

The memory was fleeting. She must have been very young, and all she really remembered was that her gram was kind, matronly, and felt safe. She remembered eating well also. Apple dumplings, peach cobbler, and vegetables straight from the garden.

Their visit had ended all too soon, and she'd never been back. But Gram had stayed in touch over the years, and she'd even come down to visit Tosha several times. Tosha would have liked to return the favor, but at first she was more interested in chasing whatever guy she was with, and then the idea of such a road trip with small children was overwhelming to undertake by herself.

Tobias probably had no idea how much easier he had made her life by coming and helping her, but to her dying day, she would be grateful. She was not going to like him, nothing more than as a very casual, very, very casual friend.

At least that's what she tried to tell herself as she tore her eyes away from him and stepped out of the car.

He was already getting River out, and she knew he would carry Phoenix in as well. She unhooked the car seat and grabbed Gemmy. Mitchell and Bailey had unhooked themselves and were waiting to get out of the back once they got the kids out of the car seats in the middle.

Sure enough, as she met Tobias at the front of the vehicle, he took Phoenix's car seat without saying anything.

"I thought your gram would be out to greet us. I texted her the last time we stopped and told her that we only had a couple of hours left. I didn't hear back from her though," he said, surprise in his voice, as though he was just realizing that she hadn't responded.

"It seems really quiet," she said, and for some reason, her words came out in a whisper. As though she were naturally trying to keep her voice down to match what was going on around her. The wind weaving through the grasses was really the only sound. From what Gram had said, the wind never stopped. It was similar to Sioux City in that regard. Only it got a lot colder up here.

And there were a lot fewer people.

"Maybe she went somewhere," she said, even as she looked at the older SUV parked alongside the house. As far as she knew, Gram only had one vehicle, plus a farm truck that was parked over by some kind of implement shed.

"No, that's the car she drives. She's here." Tobias seemed to be thoughtful as they walked up the steps.

He opened the screen door and held it with his foot since he had River in his arm and Phoenix's car seat in his other hand.

"Should I just walk in?" she asked, feeling odd asking a nonfamily member what she should do in her own gram's house.

He nodded. "Go ahead. Call out when you walk in, so she knows we're here."

She didn't have a better idea, so she just did what she was told, opening the door and calling out, "Gram! It's Tosha. The kids and I are here along with Tobias."

There was silence in the house and then a moan.

"Gram?" she said as some kind of tight band squeezed her chest.

"Here." Tobias didn't say anything more, just shoved River at her and set Phoenix down on the floor. "Wait here."

There was no question that his words were meant as a command to be obeyed to the letter. Even Mitchell didn't move.

It was a little bit cold, and Tosha would like to shut the door, but she didn't dare move. She didn't want to disobey Tobias, and if they needed to get away quickly, shutting the door would only hinder them.

What else would be making a groaning sound, other than her gram? Her gram was obviously there, since the car was there, but...had she been attacked? Did someone break into her house? There was no one else around, so no one would be able to see. There wasn't even a dog to greet them.

If she recalled correctly, in those slim memories that she had that she couldn't quite grasp all the time, she seemed to remember a dog. A shaggy one that was as tall as she was, which really wasn't very tall considering that she couldn't have been very old.

"Tosha. Call 911."

She didn't question him, but grabbed her phone out of her pocket, and dialed the emergency number.

As she held the phone to her head, she moved the car seat out of the way and motioned for the other kids to come in so she could shut the door. She assumed that if there was some kind of problem, Tobias would have commanded her to run, not call 911.

She had taken a few steps toward the hall where Tobias disappeared when the dispatcher answered. "Rockerton emergency services. How can I help you?"

"It's my gram," she began, coming upon Tobias as he knelt down on the floor at the bottom of the steps.

The crumpled person at the bottom must have been her gram. She could see white hair that seemed to have been parted and perhaps braided down her back. Her gram had long white hair? She didn't even know.

"I think she fell down the steps. It looks like she might have broken her hip. I could be wrong, but it hurts to move, and I told her to stay still."

She relayed that information to the dispatcher and confirmed the address. The dispatcher assured her that they would have an ambulance out as soon as possible. She started asking more questions, and Tosha just handed the phone to Tobias.

He answered the questions matter-of-factly, shortly, and did a few things the dispatcher suggested before he hung up and handed the phone back to her.

"This wasn't how I expected to greet you," her gram said, and those were the first words Tosha heard her say, other than answering two of Tobias's questions.

"I'm so sorry. You must be in a lot of pain." Tosha wasn't sure what to say or what to do. She knew her gram mostly through calls and texts, but she had opened up her home and invited her to stay, and she felt some responsibility, because surely she was doing something to prepare for their arrival when she had, apparently, fallen down the stairs.

"Yeah. I don't recall hurting this much since childbirth," her gram said with a wan smile.

"Don't try to move," Tobias ordered as the old woman tried to sit up.

"Watch your mouth, young man," her gram said, and there was obvious affection in her tone. Her gram and Tobias shared a bond that almost made Tosha jealous. She could see it easily as the two interacted. Tobias was completely at ease, and her gram oozed affection around the pain.

"I think I hear the sirens," Tobias said after a while. The kids had huddled in the corner, and thankfully they weren't running around yet, although Mitchell had been standing beside Tobias, close enough to touch him, but with his hands in his pockets, staring at the strange lady who lay groaning on the floor.

"I hear them too," Bailey offered.

"You want to follow her to the hospital?" he asked, looking up at Tosha with questions in his eyes.

"I better not take all of my kids to the hospital."

"I can watch them. Or if you'd like, I'll get one of my sisters to watch them, and I'll be in as soon as I can."

"What does Gram want?" she asked, not sure that her gram would even welcome her presence in the hospital.

"You guys can take care of the kids. You don't have to come in." Her words were laced with pain, and Tosha wished that there was something she could do.

"We're not going to allow you to go in by yourself. Either Tosha's going with you, or I am. Both of us can, if Tosha is okay with me calling one of my sisters."

Tosha nodded her head. Of course she was okay with it. Tobias had been nothing but trustworthy, and he had been protective of her kids. She assumed that he would not allow just anyone to watch them, and if his sisters were half as good as what he was, they would be the best babysitters her kids had ever had.

He pulled out his phone without saying anything more and punched in a number. "Stonewall. Tobias."

There was a pause.

"I need you. Mrs. Wells has fallen, and I believe she's broken something, possibly her hip. I want to follow her to the hospital, but her granddaughter is here with her five children. Can you and Joanna come and keep an eye on them while we go in to the hospital to be with Mrs. Wells?"

Stonewall didn't sound like a woman's name, but then he said Joanna, which must have been the sister he was talking about. So the sister was married? Tosha realized she knew nothing about him other than he had eleven siblings. And that he was the fourth. Why hadn't she questioned him more? She wished she knew everything about him, but now was not the time, not with her gram in so much pain and with him trying to arrange everything.

"Yes, as soon as you can get here."

She realized she probably ought to settle her kids somehow and get some things carried in, get them arranged. She set about doing that while Tobias finished his conversation and stayed with her gram.

"When the ambulance comes, you guys need to stay out of the way," she said. "You stay close to me, okay?"

The kids nodded solemnly, obviously scared. Phoenix was starting to fuss, and she realized it was way past time for him to have a bottle.

Maybe she shouldn't have agreed to go to the hospital right away. Her kids would need to be settled, she didn't even know where they were going to sleep or anything. The only way to figure it out was to get to it, so she did the best she could, bothering her gram as little as possible.

Eventually the ambulance crew arrived, and the EMTs came in, carrying the stretcher. They didn't waste any time. And she was thankful for that, for her gram's sake.

Tobias stayed with them until her gram was wheeled out and disappeared into the back of the ambulance. By that time, she had a bottle made for Phoenix and had Bailey feeding him while she carried their bags of clothes and divided them up into the rooms her gram had said were available.

It was a big old farmhouse, and there were five bedrooms upstairs. It looked like two of them were being used, and she wondered who else Gram had living with her. Maybe a hired hand? She wasn't sure. She hadn't asked and didn't want to bother her. But there were three other bedrooms, one for the boys, one for the girls, and one for her.

She'd carried the last of the clothes up when Tobias met her at the bottom of the stairs. "Sorry I wasn't able to help you. They're heading to the hospital in Rockerton. Gram has her phone, and she'll let me know where they take her."

"You don't need to apologize. I appreciate you taking care of her. She's not a relative of yours."

"No. But I suppose from all the work I've done here, I've grown fond of her. I've never seen her anything but completely capable, so it was a little disconcerting to see her unable to move and in so much pain."

"Yeah. I guess I don't know her very well."

"I think she'd like that to change."

"So now you're a good Samaritan, reuniting me with my grandma for her pleasure."

"No. I was just stating a fact." He didn't seem put off by her unprovoked attack. It was almost like he'd gotten used to her lashing out at the strangest times. She didn't know why she did it.

"I'm sorry. I didn't need to say anything like that. You certainly haven't insinuated that there are any problems that way."

"Thanks for the vote of confidence," he said, and she could hear the sarcasm in his voice.

"I think I hear a vehicle. Could that be your sister?"

"It probably is."

"Who's Stonewall?" she asked, hoping that that wasn't his sister, although she wasn't sure why. A girl could be named Stonewall; it was just unusual.

"That's Joanna's best friend. They don't do anything without each other, and I figured that having the two of them together would be better than just having one person. If you're not used to taking care of five kids, it can get a little overwhelming."

"And Stonewall might be able to handle Mitchell," she said, feeling like she had figured out what was going on.

"There's that too," he said, nodding, and perhaps he was grinning just a bit.

"You can say that. I'm not going to be offended. I understand he's a handful."

"Is that what you call him? A handful?" he said, and this time, he really was grinning.

He had been so serious, so concerned when her gram was there, and so serious on the whole trip as they drove toward Sweet Water, that this grinning man in front of her was almost foreign.

"You're happy to be home," she said, narrowing her eyes and wondering if that was really it.

He nodded. "There's nothing like North Dakota." He didn't seem to be inclined to say more, and she didn't question him. But he wasn't even from North Dakota. It made her wonder what in the world there was about this vast, wild country that made this taciturn man smile.

Before they could say anything else, there was a knock at the door. Tobias went to answer it while Tosha looked around to see what had happened to her children. The floors were wood, and the sound of the kids echoed through the house, so the only one she really needed to keep an eye on was Gemmy, who was old enough to know that she was allowed to climb stairs without her mom.

She found River and noted that Tobias had Phoenix in his arm as he opened the door.

Bailey and Mitchell followed her to the kitchen where they hung back while Tobias greeted Joanna and Stonewall.

"Appreciate you guys coming on such short notice."

"Any time. You don't usually ask for favors," Stonewall said.

"Don't let him fool you. I had to drag him here." The woman that Tosha assumed was Joanna rolled her eyes and then gave a slight grin to Stonewall.

They were best friends? They sure acted like they were great friends, but there also seemed to be an electricity between them that Tosha would almost swear meant that they were more. Maybe Tobias just didn't realize it.

"That's your sister, making things up as usual," Stonewall said, walking in and closing the door. Not looking like he had to be dragged at all.

"I don't know why I hang around you when you're so mean to me," Joanna said, smacking him on the arm.

"I'm mean to you? You're the one who insulted me as soon as we stepped in the door. I can't go anywhere without you telling everyone how terrible I am."

"I'm always telling everyone how wonderful you are. You just have such a huge ego that you can't ever get enough of that."

"So you just complimented me, and I missed it? Go ahead and say it again," Stonewall said, obviously picking on her.

The banter between the two of them was super cute, and Tosha wanted to just sit and listen to them. They were obviously messing with each other and completely and totally comfortable with each other as well. Had she ever had a friend like that? Certainly she'd never had a relationship like that with either one of her husbands and never with any of her boyfriends either. In fact, their relationships had been more fights than anything.

"I'll let Tosha go through the instructions for the kids, and then she and I are going to run. You probably passed the ambulance."

"We did. It was trucking along pretty good." Stonewall took his hat and coat off and hung them over the back of a chair in the kitchen. Joanna handed him hers, and he hung it over top of his.

They seemed to know what the other was going to do without any communication passing between them at all.

"I don't have a whole lot to say. Phoenix just had a bottle. And he'll need to be changed at least once more before he goes to bed. I have all of his stuff in the baby bag right here," she said, pointing to the chair where she set the baby bag. "The pack and play is set up in the bedroom. And I guess when the kids get tired, you can put them to bed. I was going to put the girls in the room upstairs with the yellow walls, and I was going to put the boys in the room with the wooden walls." She didn't figure it mattered, other than yellow seemed more girly than brown so that was how she was going to divide it up.

"Have they eaten?" Joanna asked.

She told them what time they ate and said that they probably would need to have supper, but she didn't have anything prepared and they had just arrived. Joanna waved her off.

"Don't worry about it. We're really good at making ourselves at home, and I know Mrs. Wells will be totally fine with us using her kitchen. I hope she feels better."

"Me too," Tosha said, and she felt like she and Joanna could be friends. She thought maybe she was a little bit older than Joanna, but not much, although their life experiences would have been completely different.

"Are you ready to go then?" Tobias said. He didn't seem to be impatient. He didn't seem to be pushing her. He was just asking. Although, she knew he cared greatly for her grandmother and wanted to get to the hospital. He was willing to wait for her until she was ready.

She thought back through her life, trying to remember if she'd ever been with someone who didn't want her to be on his timeline all the time.

It was her gram, she should be pushing to leave, but she hated to get to a new place and leave her children.

Still, Joanna and Stonewall seemed very responsible, and Tobias obviously trusted them. And her grandma obviously loved Tobias. There was a warmth and friendship between them that was unexpected.

"I am," she said, walking over to him and taking one last look at her children. They didn't seem to be afraid, although they were watching her with big eyes.

"You guys be good and be as helpful as you can to Mr. Stonewall and Miss Joanna, okay?"

They nodded their heads, and even Mitchell seemed like he was going to obey. Had Tobias said something to him?

She would be curious to see if he had, but she didn't ask as he opened the door and she walked out, curious to see what would go on with her grandmother at the hospital and hoping she would be totally fine.

Chapter Twelve

Tobias walked in the hospital, going straight to the nurses' station since the information desk was closed for the evening. He gave the name of Mrs. Wells and waited to see what they would say.

"Are you a relative?"

"I'm her granddaughter," Tosha spoke up before he could answer. He wasn't a relative, and maybe he shouldn't be allowed in, but the nurse didn't question them anymore. She simply nodded and told him that she didn't have a room and she was still in the emergency room. She gave them directions, and they walked along the hall.

"It didn't even occur to me that they wouldn't let me in if I wasn't related," Tobias said.

"You could lie." The words were said softly, easily, but they almost made Tobias recoil.

"No. I'm not going to lie. I wouldn't do it."

Maybe she hesitated just a moment in one of her steps, but she quickly caught herself and continued on. "Really? You wouldn't lie for anything?"

"Never say never. I'm human. But lying is wrong, whether it's to get something you want or to circumvent a rule you think is ridiculous, like only relatives being allowed to see patients in the hospital. It's just... wrong."

"Do you really live by that?"

"By what?"

"By everything the Bible says. I assume that's why you don't lie. Because Jesus told us not to."

"Did Jesus command it? I just know it's a command in the Bible, but God abhors lying. It's an abomination to Him. I don't want anything I do to be an abomination to the Lord."

"Because you're afraid He's going to strike you with lightning?"

She seemed to have a chip on her shoulder about the Lord. About Christians in general.

Lord? Are You sure this is the woman You want me to have? He really did believe that it was not right for Christians to marry non-Christians. The Bible clearly said that Christians were not to be unequally yoked with unbelievers. To him, that was obviously talking about marriage. And he didn't believe that God would tell him to do something that went against the Bible. But there was the example of Hosea. Of course, Hosea was a prophet. Still, that didn't negate the fact that he felt strongly that the Lord wanted him to offer marriage.

Maybe He knew that Tosha was going to refuse. That was the only out he could see.

"No. Because I love God, and when you love someone, you don't want to grieve them or do things that would make them sad. I also feel like I was bought with a price. The death of Jesus. I owe him my very life. And the Bible says that I'm to present my body as a living sacrifice to the Lord, which is the least that I can do in return for what He's done for me."

"I feel like you really believe that stuff."

"I do."

"I guess no one really ever explained that to me. I... I made a confession of faith when I was a little girl, but it seemed like God hated me, because every time I turned around, something terrible happened."

"Because of God? Or because of your poor choices?" He didn't really want to say that. She was allowed to get mad at him. After all, no one wanted to say that they made choices. But to his surprise, she laughed.

"You're not mincing any words, are you?"

"You're blaming God for things that aren't His fault."

"I guess you would be hard-pressed to convince me that God wants bad things to happen to people who are basically good."

"You think you're basically good?"

"Aren't you?"

"No. My heart is desperately wicked and deceitful. If I did what I am, I would be lying when I felt like it, sleeping around, and cheating on whoever I was sleeping with."

"All right. I guess that all sounds familiar. And I've seen that in non-Christians. In my experience."

"And?"

"And you are different, but I know a lot of Christians who aren't."

"Maybe there are a lot of Christians who claim to be Christians but don't really live what they say they believe."

"Yeah. Maybe that's me."

"So you're Christian?" He tried to keep the hope out of his voice.

"I told you, I made a profession of faith when I was younger."

"And?"

"And I guess I always believed, and you're right. I knew that a lot of times the things that happened to me were a result of my poor choices, not because God was punishing me. But there are things that have happened to me and things that happened to people that I have seen that are hard to explain if God really is a God of love."

By that time, they had reached the waiting room and the reception area where the receptionist told them to have a seat and she would call them back when Mrs. Wells was ready to receive visitors. She said the doctors were working on her currently.

They settled in, and he wondered if he should pick up the conversation where they left off. Then he figured, why not?

"So if God is a God of love, why does He allow bad things to happen?"

"Do you have an answer?" She turned her head, surprise in her eyes and voice.

"Not a good one, but is it not because of man's sin? When Adam chose to disobey, sin entered the world, and God allowed it to. He didn't stop it, although He could have."

"Why didn't He?"

"I'm not sure. But I know that a lot of times when bad things happen to people, God ends up turning around and using those terrible things to somehow bless other people. If you look at Job."

"That's the one who lost everything? Including his ten children?"

"Yeah. You wonder how can someone losing his ten children work out for good?"

"Yeah. How did it?"

She seemed genuinely interested, and he chose his words carefully.

"Well, millions of us have read the story of Job. We've seen that God allowed Satan to tempt Job, because God knew that Job would show Satan that he could still praise God, even in the midst of all suffering. And Job did. And for those of us who read his story, we can find encouragement in the fact that nothing happened to Job without God's allowing it to. And even in the midst of all that, God protected Job and ended up blessing him with more than he had before."

"So God allowed it so other people could be encouraged?"

"I think so. And so we can see that God has our best interest at heart in everything. Even though sometimes it's hard to see. After all, losing a loved one is one of the hardest things that can happen, but if we think about it, it's really not a bad thing, is it? If they go to heaven? Why would we begrudge them being able to spend eternity in heaven with Jesus? Wouldn't we be happy for them if we were really thinking about it from a perspective of wanting the best for them and not necessarily the best for ourselves? Isn't our grief a little bit selfish on our part because we want them with us?"

"But they might have suffered."

"Once you're through the suffering, you don't remember it. All you remember is how happy you currently are."

She seemed to be thinking about that for a moment, as she tried to test whether his words were true. "I guess it's a little bit like labor. It feels like you're going to die, and sometimes I wanted to, but when they put the baby in your arms, you forget all about it."

"Going to heaven must be a million times better, wouldn't it?"

"I suppose so."

She seemed to be thinking, and he didn't interrupt her. He supposed he really didn't have a great answer to why God allowed suffering in the world. Other than mankind had allowed sin to enter the world, so they were kind of getting what their fathers had allowed in. But at some point, everything would be avenged. And the world would be made right. It was that happy ending that enabled him to look past the suffering of the current world and know that God would make everything right in the end. He really didn't understand how that could happen, how all the atrocities in the world could somehow be made right, but if God said it was possible, then it was just Tobias's job to believe.

"I think sometimes it just seems so impossible for us that we can't imagine how it could possibly happen, but if God says it, it's not really our job to figure it out. That's where faith comes in. The faith of a little child. We just believe, we don't question, we don't try to figure it out, we don't think that is impossible or anything like that. We just trust, blindly and completely."

"I found that trusting blindly and completely is dangerous."

"Not when that trust is in God."

Tobias wanted to say more, but just then the nurse walked in and said, "Family for Mrs. Wells?"

"I'm the granddaughter," Tosha said immediately, standing. Tobias stood beside her, wanting to support her if she needed it. Mrs. Wells had been talking before she got in the ambulance and seemed to have some kind of pain that Tobias hoped was just a broken bone and not some kind of internal injury. Although, at Mrs. Wells's age, a broken bone could spell just as much trouble as internal injuries could.

"We've been able to do an X-ray, and her hip is fractured. There isn't a whole lot we can do with it, other than treat her for the pain and keep her comfortable. We didn't see any other injuries, although the doc is still going to run some more tests. If one of you would like to go back and see her, you can come with me. We do ask for just one at a time, since it's rather busy tonight."

Tosha looked at Tobias, and he nodded his head, indicating she could go back. He could sit here and pray and didn't need to sit with Mrs. Wells. Although he hated that Tosha would be there by herself. It seemed like she had been doing a lot by herself, raising her five kids, struggling to survive all on her own. Of course, he wasn't going to pretend that a lot of the choices that had led her to be doing that on her own weren't hers. Still, sometimes a person made bad decisions and learned from their mistakes, but they still had a hole to dig out of. It seemed like maybe that was what Tosha was doing, and perhaps that was why the Lord had sent him along to help. It also seemed like she wasn't completely closed to the idea of being a Christian, and she'd admitted that she made a decision for the Lord when she was younger but had walked away from it.

Lord, are You going to use this to bring her back to You? How do I fit into it?

He still couldn't shake the idea that God wanted him to propose marriage, but he needed to be up-front with her. He couldn't pretend that it was for romantic reasons. Although, he hoped they would grow into them.

Maybe it was just wishful thinking on his part. He sat back down as Tosha gave him one more glance and walked away behind the nurse, following her around the corner and out of sight.

Chapter Thirteen

Tosha walked into her grandma's room, smiling at the nurse who nodded silently and then waited for Tosha to walk in before she slipped back out.

Gram looked old and tired as she lay in bed, and very small. It had been years since Tosha had seen her, and somehow in her mind, she was vibrant and, if not young, at least middle-aged, with a warm smile. Capable and bustling around. She smelled of cinnamon and vanilla and always had her arms wide open for a hug.

But now, with her eyes closed and her body so still, Tosha felt more like she was the adult and the caretaker.

She supposed that was a role she would embrace, if that was what it came to. But it was unexpected, and she felt a little unsteady as she walked into the room and put her hand over top of Gram's cold one.

"Gram?"

The lady's eyes fluttered and then opened, seeming to move a bit before they focused on Tosha.

"Tosha?" her gram said quietly.

"It's me," Tosha said, nodding.

"Sorry. I didn't mean to fall down the steps and ruin our reunion."

"You didn't ruin anything. And I know you didn't mean to fall down the stairs," Tosha said, not knowing what else to say. She tugged her chair closer and sat down. Close enough that she could look into Gram's eyes and they were a little bit more on level.

"Did you bring all the kids? I didn't really get to see them before when you all came in. I guess they were scared of the old lady who was crumpled in a heap on the floor."

Her words were a bit slurred, almost as though she had been given pain medication and it was working.

"Yeah. Tobias called his sister and her friend to come watch them."

"Tobias. Has he asked you to marry him yet?"

Tosha gasped and recoiled, even though she didn't mean to. What was Gram talking about? Was that what Tobias actually wanted? But that was crazy. "I just met him yesterday," Tosha said, gently, not wanting to make Gram feel bad for not knowing what she was talking about because of the medication.

Her gram looked at her, and her eyes held pain, but they were clear and obviously not confused. "You might have just met him yesterday, but we've been talking about you for a while. And he has every intention of proposing marriage."

Tasha didn't understand. It didn't make any sense. Why would he be proposing marriage? What was her gram saying that would make him feel like he had to? It wasn't like the man was madly in love with her or anything. He had been, well, not exactly formal, but definitely not too familiar or any of the other signs that she'd come to expect from men who were interested in her. And she had a bit of experience.

Gram had to be mistaken, although Tosha almost wanted to hold onto the dream and think that she was actually right, that a man as respectable and full of character as Tobias was might actually be interested in her.

"Are there animals who need to be fed while you're laid up?" Tosha asked, figuring that the change of subject would be wise. Gram seemed tired and weak, and while it seemed like the pain meds were doing a good job, her mouth and eyes still seemed tight and she looked tense.

"Yes. Tobias knows."

How would Tobias know? Were he and her gram really that great of friends?

"Is he your hired help?"

"He doesn't let me pay him," Gram said with a small smile. "It would be hard to find a better man."

Tosha already would have said that Tobias was a good man, and hearing her gram say that only confirmed what she had been thinking during the car ride here.

But he was still a man. And she had sworn off men.

"Is there anything I can do?" she asked, squeezing her gram's hand and truly wanting to help this woman who had opened up her home when she had nowhere else to go and sent this man, one that seemed to be almost too good to be true, to go get her.

"Just take care of Tobias," Gram said, somehow sounding more weary than she had just a few moments before.

"Of course," Tosha replied, not sure exactly what her gram meant by that. Being that Tobias was her hired man, it seemed that he would be the one taking care of them.

She felt just a little disconcerted. This conversation wasn't going the way she expected it to, and the reunion with her gram had definitely gotten thrown off the rails. Still, her gram obviously was not unhappy to have her, and it made her feel welcome in her home, even if Gram wasn't going to be there.

"Excuse me. If you don't mind going back out to the waiting room for a while, we need to take her back to do some more tests." A nurse, not the one who had come to get her just a few moments ago, came to the door and stuck her head in.

"Of course," Tosha said, looking at the nurse before she turned back to her gram. "I'll be out in the waiting room. And I'll be back in here as soon as they allow me to."

"Thank you, child."

Gram weakly squeezed her fingers before Tosha slipped her hand out and slid away from the side of the bed. She took one last look, hearing the beeping of the machine and the clacking of the bed as the nurse adjusted the controls, probably intending to wheel her gram out on it.

It wasn't hard to leave the emergency area and find the waiting room, where Tobias sat in the chair, his forearms on his knees, his hands clasped between them. His head was bowed, almost as though he were praying. He definitely did not look like he was relaxed, but he didn't look irritated or upset, either. Most of the men that she had been with over the years would have been irritated that she had gone back and he had not been able to, anxious to leave, and bored sitting in the waiting room. Possibly even angry.

Tobias didn't look any of those things.

"She's in pain, but they have her on meds and she looks a lot more comfortable than she did."

"That's great," he said, his head coming up as soon as she started talking, as though he hadn't heard her approach.

"They're taking her back for more tests, so they sent me back out here. If they come to get someone again, you can go back."

"You're her granddaughter, and you haven't seen her for a long time. I know she was really looking forward to your visit. This is definitely not how she expected to greet you."

"No. She said that." She glanced at the chair beside him and then decided she would sit down before she broached the subject she felt she needed to.

He shifted as she sat down, moving his body so that it was angled toward her a bit and leaning back in his chair, setting an ankle on his knee.

There were other people in the waiting room, but they were the only ones in this corner. A TV, tuned to a house makeover show, droned on in the background. Some of the families spoke quietly together, and there were several people who sat by themselves.

This wasn't the best place for her to bring up what her grandma said, but...it was where they were.

"What's bothering you?" Tobias asked, almost as though he could read her mind. She'd never been with anyone who was even the slightest bit good at reading minds. Most of the time, the men she was with expected her to read theirs and couldn't care less about hers.

"Gram said that you were planning on asking me to marry you. I thought it was the drugs talking. She seemed a little bit sleepy, and I thought maybe she was confused. But she seemed pretty sincere, so I figured I would just ask you. Why would she say something like that? And then, she told me to take care of you. I thought that was odd too. I mean, I understand you're her hired hand, but it's not like...there's anything I can do to take care of you in that role."

Tobias looked at her for a few moments and didn't seem surprised about anything that she told him, even though she felt the information she was relaying was rather shocking.

Finally he lifted a large shoulder and said, "I'm not sure why she would tell you to take care of me. But maybe no one told you that I've been living with your gram. I do have a cabin of my own adjacent to the property my family owns, Sweet View Ranch. But your gram has been getting older and more feeble, and I didn't want her to be alone in case she fell." There was irony on his face as he spoke, acknowledging that what he had tried to prevent from happening had happened anyway.

"It's not your fault you weren't there," Tosha said immediately, seeing that he felt guilty too.

"I know. But she's just...getting older, and she is not used to slowing down. I was better able to help her from her house, and I asked if I could rent a room. There were lots of rooms that weren't being used at the time."

"Yeah. But now that I'm there, we filled them all out."

"I can move out."

He said the words so easily, like he was willing to do whatever it took to make her happy. But somehow those words reminded her of the other thing that her gram had said, that he had not addressed.

"Why would Gram have told me that you were going to ask me to marry you? We had never even met before yesterday."

His lips tightened, and he met her eyes before glancing around the room. "There is a little prayer room just off the main waiting room here. Do you mind if we go there to talk for a moment?"

Tosha's heart stopped beating for just a few moments. And then, when it started, it seemed to rush all at once to catch up for what it missed. After all, he should have vehemently denied that he planned to ask her to marry him, and he didn't.

"Of course," she finally managed to say, although the sound of her voice shocked her. Or maybe it was just her nerves were all of a sudden ultrasensitive. He didn't deny it. But... Why? And did he know her from somewhere that she had no clue about? But that didn't explain why he would think that she would actually say yes to such a crazy proposal. Surely he didn't think that just because she had five children she was willing to take the next man who threw himself into her path.

Of course, when she was younger and less wise, she certainly would have. Maybe he didn't realize that she'd grown up since then. That her children were now her main concern, and caring for them and providing for them and helping her gram were the things that she was going to focus on.

Of course he wouldn't know that. After all, her history certainly pointed to the fact that she jumped from man to man to man with absolutely no standards or values at all. But Tobias had been right in his choices. He'd chosen to be pure until he found the one who was right for him. How she wished she would have done the same. But it was too late for her to go back and change anything, though not too late for her to move forward on a different path.

Still, she would go to the prayer room, trusting that Tobias did not have any bad intentions, and hear what he had to say.

They walked slowly and silently across the room. The people who sat there glanced up as they walked by but didn't say anything.

Tobias opened the door and held it for her, and they walked into the small room. There was a cross on the table, something that she assumed were rosary beads, and a couple of chairs around the table as well as a loveseat along the wall. There was a dim light in the ceiling, and the whole place just gave off an aura of calm and peace.

"Want to sit here?" Tobias asked, indicating the loveseat.

Her heart was still thundering, and she tried to get a handle on her breath as she gave the loveseat a glance.

"I think I'd rather sit at the table if you don't mind." She didn't want to be on the loveseat and have him make some kind of unexpected advance. Not that Tobias had been anything but an extreme gentleman to her, and he had not shown the slightest proclivity toward doing anything untoward, but she'd been in more situations than she cared to admit where she had a man making advances that were unwelcome.

"That's fine," Tobias said, and he didn't seem to be offended that she didn't choose to sit where he wanted her to. He simply held a chair for her and then pulled out the other chair, which was at an angle from hers.

"I have something to tell you that is going to sound...crazy."

"More crazy than my gram telling me a man that I had never met before in my entire life until yesterday was going to ask me to marry him? I find that hard to believe."

He lifted a shoulder. "Believe it. This is going to be pretty amazing."

"All right. I'm listening."

"About three weeks or so ago, I got a letter in the mail. It was from a lawyer's office that I didn't recognize and had never heard of. It talked about someone who had left a legacy in Sweet Water and who was giving out money for people to get married."

"Giving out money for people to get married?" She couldn't help but interrupt him. That was crazy. "Like paying for the wedding or something?"

Tobias shook his head. "Not unless you're going to spend one billion dollars on the wedding."

"One million?"

"No. Billion. With a B. That's nine hundred, ninety-nine million, plus one more million."

"Oh my goodness. That's...so much money."

"Yeah. Now, about three hundred thirty-three million would go to taxes if you actually got that much money, so it's not quite as much as what you think." He said that with a turned-up lip, which would seem to be his idea of smiling, and Tosha got the impression that was the way he smiled.

"All right, six hundred sixty-six million is still a lot of money."

"Agreed."

"All right, that's great. We agree on something."

He snorted. "Well, I wasn't sure whether the letter was legit or not, but this letter had references and told me I could go ask a couple of men in town that I highly respect. So I did."

"Men who live in Sweet Water?"

"Yes. Ford Hansen and Sawyer Olson are two men who lived here long before I moved here and who are highly respected in town. I met them both at the diner, and they told me that the letter was legit as far as they knew. They had both received such a letter themselves thirty years ago. And they had gotten the money just as the letter said because they both got married in that timeframe."

"What is the timeframe?" Tosha asked, thinking that it must have been five years so two people could find each other and date long enough to fall in love.

"One month from the date of the letter."

"One month?" she repeated, knowing she was parroting him, but it sounded unbelievable.

"That's right. And I got the letter three and a half weeks ago."

"That means you have...a couple of days to get married?"

Tobias nodded. "At first, I just dismissed the letter. After all, I don't have anyone I'm interested in getting married to, and I've always been very careful. I guess you and I talked about that a little bit. I'm not interested in getting married to someone who isn't going to stay with me for the rest of my life or who isn't a Christian and isn't interested in living for the Lord."

"I see. You mentioned that you needed kissing lessons."

If she wasn't mistaken, there was a flush underneath his tan. It was adorable, and she would have smiled about it if she hadn't been so... thrown off by everything he was saying. If her gram hadn't admired him so much, if he hadn't been so respectable, if her gut wasn't telling her he was trustworthy, she would definitely have dismissed it out of hand. But those three reasons kept her listening.

"I did. I guess we talked about that some too. I suppose I knew that I was going to be having this conversation with you at some point, and I wanted you to know exactly what I am. I'm probably not what you're used to."

He said it in such a way that it made it sound like he knew that he wasn't as good as the men she was normally with, when the exact opposite was true. She'd never been with anyone who didn't know how to kiss.

"You're definitely not what I'm used to. I've never met anyone who was as quiet and calm as you are, to begin with."

"I've actually talked more today than I normally talk. I... I guess I don't always know exactly what to say."

"That's okay. There's nothing wrong with that. I guess some people spout off a lot of words and never mean anything, so there's the other end of the spectrum which is, in my opinion, worse."

Chapter Fourteen

Tobias jerked his head and ran a hand over his hair before he set it back down on the table, steepling his fingers together.

"When your gram mentioned that she had invited you to come live with her because you were losing your apartment, and then she started talking about how you'd been through a lot of hard things and how she wished her farm had been making more money so that she could help you out. That raising five children was hard and that you and she had been talking and you had been thinking about how you needed to turn your life around."

"I have been. I was shying away from Christianity, because I'm a little bit annoyed at God. But you have such a rock-solid faith." She narrowed her eyes, trying to put her finger on what exactly it was about him that made her shift in direction. "I guess it's just really hard to be around you and not feel like everything that you think is exactly right. I've never met anyone who was so sure about God. Not like you are."

"God's Word has been right, over and over and over again. And I suppose back when I was younger, I dug into the facts. I wanted to make sure that the Bible was true and that I could trust it. I wanted to know if Jesus really lived, and if salvation through faith in His shed blood was actually the way to heaven."

"Did you figure it out?" She couldn't help her curious question.

"I did. I looked up a lot of different things. Probably the main one is the fact that almost all historians agree that Jesus was an actual man who lived exactly when the Bible says he did. There are writings, outside the Bible, plus the Bible itself, and four different books by four different men that all agree. And then that leads you to the question, why would a man, who was poor and nondescript, still be talked about two thousand years after he walked the earth, unless there was something very special about that man?"

"Because he made up a bunch of lies and people believed them." She was playing devil's advocate a little bit, but that seemed like a plausible explanation to her.

"Okay. Say that's true. One of his disciples betrayed him, but eleven of the twelve disciples who walked the earth with him, after his resurrection, all died martyr's deaths, except one, John, who was boiled in oil as a martyr but survived."

"They have to really believe in order to suffer like that, I suppose."

"Yeah. They suffered truly terrible things but always continued to try to spread the gospel wherever they went. They knew that by believing in Christ and preaching him to other people, earthly suffering and gruesome death would be their fate. Christians were fed to the lions, crucified, used as living lamps, and sawn in pieces, along with the boiling in oil. I wouldn't go through something like that unless I really believed what it was I said I believed."

"Me either."

"So what they believed was that Jesus was who he said he was, that he died and rose from the dead. That he is the Son of God. Plus, there are a lot of facts and history that support the resurrection, and most scholars agree it happened. There were more than five hundred people who saw Jesus die and then saw him walk the earth after his death. The Roman soldiers even pierced his side with the sword to make sure that he was dead. There was no doubt about it. He was dead, and he came back to life."

"That's pretty compelling."

"Yeah. And then of course, back in those days, women didn't really have a good position in society."

"I know. I'm thankful I live today."

"They just weren't really considered important. And yet the Bible has women finding the empty tomb and realizing that Jesus had risen. The angel spoke with them. It's interesting that that's who did it. If someone was making the story up, they would have someone important finding the empty tomb, right?"

"Yeah. I guess if you're making a story up, you can make it be however you want it to be, and you put the best person possible as the most credible witness."

"Exactly. But they weren't making the story up, they were telling the truth, and the first witnesses were women. That's what's recorded in the Bible, and that's one of the things that, while it doesn't conclusively say that it's true, it points to the idea that it was, since who is going to make up a lie that makes them look bad?"

"It's sad that women finding the empty tomb would make anyone look bad."

"That's not how we believe today, but I don't think that's how God leads. After all, He could have had anyone find the empty tomb and talk to the angel, but he had women doing it. To me, that shows that God honors and respects women. Although He does have specific roles for women in the home."

"Yeah. Barefoot and pregnant." Tosha rolled her eyes.

"Is it such a bad thing to bring new life into the world?" Tobias had a point, but Tosha wasn't really in the mood to give him more than the points he'd already earned. His defense of the resurrection was on point. He didn't exactly address her doubts, because she hadn't articulated exactly what bothered her about believing. Was it the fact that she would have to change? Maybe it wasn't that she really didn't believe that it happened, as much as she didn't want to have to change her life because it had. But when confronted with facts and having them pointed out in such a logical way, she could hardly deny that it happened and that for her to do anything but believe went against logic.

"I guess it's not, but when you have to do it by yourself, and you have to take care of all the other new lives you brought into the world and don't really have a home or family, and you're struggling to survive, you get tired."

That was a little bit more on point and less about what they had been discussing.

"That's why God wants a man and woman to parent together. I even think that perhaps the way we do things in our modern society, where a man and a woman live in their own house, rather than in a multigenerational house, might not be the best way. After all, if you have a set of grandparents around to give you a hand, it's not nearly so hard."

"Really? You think you would live with your parents?" She'd never heard anyone say anything like that before, and it was especially surprising coming from someone like Tobias who seemed so self-contained and capable.

"Just an idea. I mean, can't we question the way we do things and think about whether or not they're the best way?"

"I suppose we can. It's just so...radical."

"There's nothing wrong with being radical, as long as you're being radical in the right way."

"I suppose that's true too. Although I hadn't thought about it like that before. Radical seems to mean radical going in a direction other than a conservative direction. But I suppose you could be radically conservative."

"Yes. You could be radically anything, I suppose."

"So I don't mean to change the subject, but you were talking about a letter and one billion dollars and getting married, and somehow we got off track."

"Yeah. I think it started with kissing lessons, and it's kind of crazy that we went from kissing to the resurrection."

"It is, isn't it?"

He gave her a small smile, and she was captured by the handsomeness of his face when it relaxed in happiness.

She shook her head and looked away. No. She wasn't going to allow the fact that she felt so at ease with this man to make her give up what she had vowed to do, which was give up men.

She would not walk away from her vow.

He shifted in his seat as though he were uncomfortable. "So the gist of the letter was if I get married and my wife and I stay in North Dakota, we'll be given one billion dollars."

She couldn't help it. She gasped. One billion dollars just to get married and live in North Dakota.

"So, I knew that you were coming, your grandma talked about how you have struggled, and I knew that she was struggling as well. My family also has had some setbacks. I showed you the ranch where my eleven siblings live."

"I still can't believe you have eleven siblings. Wow."

He smiled, casually, almost as though that was a reaction he often got.

"There have been different things happening, and I can go into detail with them if you want me to. But I guess... I guess I was thinking that you could use a husband, your children can use a father, and both of us could use the money for different things. I was definitely thinking of helping your grandma, but I also wanted to help my family and make sure that you are set up."

"How long do we have to stay married?" That seemed like a reasonable question to her. They had to live in North Dakota, but they could agree to get married for a year, and then he could divorce her and be rid of her.

"For the rest of our lives. That's what marriage is." He seemed a little confused that she would even have asked the question.

She was shocked that he would even consider marrying someone he didn't love and expect to spend the rest of his life with her.

"You would marry someone you didn't love and spend the rest of your life with that person, and give up the opportunity to possibly fall in love and get married like everyone else does?"

"How did falling in love and getting married work out for you?" He didn't seem accusatory, and he hadn't shifted, he just lifted his eyes, keeping his hands steepled on the table, and seemed to be patiently waiting for her answer.

This question took her aback.

"Just because my husbands didn't stay with me doesn't mean that everyone who falls in love and gets married has the same experience."

"Wouldn't it be better to get married to someone who is as

committed as you are to having a relationship for the rest of your lives? Someone who is on the same page with raising children and having children and with loving God and serving Jesus and making sure that you will stay together no matter what. Like when you say 'for better or for worse' in your vows, you actually mean it."

She kept her mouth closed. She hadn't met anyone who actually meant it when he said "for worse." It seemed like the "for better" was pretty easy, but when something hard came along, the first thing that anyone did was say, "We'll just get divorced."

"The idea of not falling in love and getting married is just too foreign."

"That's not really how anyone has done it until modern day. Up until that, you might have found out who you were going to marry on your wedding day or a little bit before, and you had to figure out how to build a relationship with that person and make a life with them. The idea of getting divorced was unheard of. Or at least had a lot of stigma associated with it."

Right. She had never thought about it that way before, but he was absolutely right. Still, the idea of falling in love had been so ingrained that it was hard for her to wrap her head around the idea that might not be the best way.

"So I guess what I'm saying is, if you'll have me, I'd like to marry you."

Chapter Fifteen

Talk about a backhanded marriage proposal. Tobias wanted to slap himself on the forehead. He couldn't have asked her in a worse way if he had tried. He couldn't have scripted a more clumsy, ridiculous marriage proposal.

"I'm sorry. That was...really terrible. I've never done this before." He tried to smile at her and make a little joke, but as soon as the words were out of his mouth and he saw the reaction on her face, and he realized that while he hadn't done it before, she had, and that's the way she was taking his words. That she had experience.

"I didn't mean it like that," he said, realizing he was making a bad situation worse. But he wasn't quite sure how to dig out of the hole that he had jumped into.

He wanted to wipe his hands on his jeans since they were sweating so bad. But he tried to make himself stay relaxed. If this was truly what the Lord wanted, the way he figured it was, her answer didn't matter. And if the money was the most important thing to him, then he had no business asking her to begin with. Sure, he'd be helping her, and he'd be helping himself and his family and Mrs. Wells. There were a lot of people who could benefit from them doing this. But the main reason that he had decided to go ahead with this proposal was because he thought it was what the Lord wanted him to do.

"I swore off men."

Her voice was soft, tiny in the small room, barely audible, and he almost leaned forward to try to catch it, to absorb what she was saying.

"That's a no?" he finally asked, running her words over in his head and unable to come up with any other idea.

"Do you have a minute?" she asked, looking around the room like she had just remembered where they were.

"Yes. Until they come in to tell us about your grandma."

"They might let us both go unless it's still as busy, but until they come back for us, can I tell you something?"

That was the second time she asked. He'd thought them sitting here together talking was invitation enough that they could chat with each other.

He nodded. "You can tell me anything."

She forced her lips back into a smile. It was obviously meant to try to make light of what she was going to say.

When she spoke, her voice was soft but firm, like she was forcing the words out and needed them to get as far away from her as possible without her raising her voice. "You said that you needed kissing lessons, and you seem to be a little bit insecure about it."

"Was it that obvious?" he asked, embarrassed that she could see right through him.

"Don't be embarrassed. I admire what you've done, the way you've lived, the decisions you made that I didn't. I ended up quitting school without getting a diploma. My mom insisted that I would regret not finishing school, but I thought she was wrong. Now I know better."

"I think all of us have not done what our parents wanted us to do at some point, and regretted it. I know I had to tell my parents that they were right more than once."

"She's gone, and I can't tell her that she's right, unfortunately."

"I'm sorry. I know it doesn't help anything, but my parents were killed in a car accident and I can't tell them that they're right about anything again."

"I got pregnant, then I got married. I had it backward."

"That happens sometimes."

But she pursed her lips and shook her head. "It happens, but it shouldn't. We got married because we thought it was the right thing to do, and then after I had Mitchell, I got pregnant with Bailey right away. She's barely thirteen months younger than him. I was divorced before she was one week old."

"That's hard."

"Yeah. He got tired of me complaining about being pregnant, about my back hurting, about how I had to go to the bathroom all the time and with a screaming baby on top of all that." Her voice trailed off a little, as though she were thinking about the things that she could have done differently.

"You shouldn't blame yourself. If he made vows, it shouldn't have mattered how much you were complaining, or the baby was crying, or anything else that was going wrong."

"He had a girlfriend." She said it casually, like every husband had a girlfriend.

"That's wrong." He wasn't sure what else to say. She did know it, and surely she had at the time.

"Yeah. Well, I might have pitched a fit or two about that."

"Understandably."

"No one likes a shrew. That's pretty much what I was. I'm not saying that I shouldn't have or that any of that was okay, I'm just saying... Yeah, he cheated, and he was grumpy and mean at times, but I was no picnic to live with either. I saw that later, but not at the time. At the time, I thought I was right because he was wrong. I guess having him be wrong automatically made me right, and whatever I did was okay."

"Cheating is just wrong. You can't paint it any other way."

"No. You're right. But I still have to take some blame, because I wasn't perfect."

"No one is."

Maybe he was defending her too much, but he believed what he was saying. A man shouldn't cheat. A woman shouldn't nag and complain. They had made vows. They were building a life together, they had a family together. If they were in an exclusive relationship of any kind, cheating was wrong, and that was the way it was.

"Anyway, our divorce was barely final before I moved in with someone else. It was like I couldn't live without a man. I needed to have a man to help me, someone to make me feel like I was beautiful, desirable, and someone to take care of me, I don't know what it was." She closed her eyes and shook her head, and he felt like she was pulling back a little curtain into her soul. He would never have thought that someone who looked the way she did could need anything. She seemed very independent and confident.

"Anyway, I was pregnant again when my second husband walked out. And then when Phoenix came along, I was living with a guy I shouldn't have been, and he asked me to move out before I even knew I was pregnant. He had someone else he wanted to move in in my place. I guess I should have expected that. But at that point in time, I knew I had to get a hold of my life. I had been making mistake after mistake after mistake, and my children were the ones who were paying for it. So that's when I vowed that I was giving up men. I wasn't going to need them for my self-esteem. I wasn't going to depend on them to make me feel attractive and pretty. In fact, it didn't matter whether I felt any of those things. I needed to look at my kids, see what they needed, and then try to provide that for them."

"They need a dad."

His words were soft, and maybe he shouldn't have said that, but she was basically telling him that while she wasn't blaming the men in her life for all of her problems, she was going to stop being with any men in order to fix the problems that she had created. But she was leaving out an important point, and he felt like she needed to hear it.

"They have three different dads, and none of them are interested. In fact, by the time I had Phoenix, I had learned that it's best to just not put their names on the birth certificate, because it might be easier to get child support, but they might fight for custody and I'd rather not have them fight, because I have a tendency to pick the very worst kind of men. I think River and Gemmy's dad is in jail right now. And Mitchell and Bailey's dad is an addict. Every once in a while, he calls me asking for money." She rolled her eyes.

His heart hurt for her. It had been a difficult life. She learned some hard lessons. But it sounded like she was headed mostly in the right direction.

"So... You know you need to make some changes."

"That's what I said. That's why any proposal of marriage is going to be met with a no from me. I wanted you to know it had nothing to do with you and everything to do with what I said I was going to do."

"Which was give up men. Not need them to make you feel attractive or desirable."

"Exactly."

"You don't have to need me. We can just get married because it's the practical thing to do. Wouldn't that be different than what you had done before?" He knew he shouldn't be arguing. If she wanted to say no, that was up to her. It wasn't up to him to talk her into it, but he couldn't stop himself, because her idea was so messed up.

"I guess it would be. But it's still marriage. It's still me going down that road again, the road I promised myself and my kids I wouldn't do."

She glanced around the room and then lowered her voice even more. He leaned closer so he could hear.

"I was stupid when I was younger." She huffed out a breath. "I mean, that's putting it mildly. I didn't think about my children first. I mean, they were kind of in the way of getting what I wanted. I'm ashamed to say it, because that sounds so terrible. But it was true. For some reason, being admired by whatever man was in my life at the time was the most important thing. I resented my kids for getting between me and that man. But as men have come and gone, and my kids are still here, and I get a little older and maybe just a little bit wiser," she smiled a bit, as though the idea of her being wise was funny, "and through all that I guess I've seen that the most important thing isn't how people see me, isn't how men in particular see me, it's what I'm doing for my children. That's where my focus needs to be. And yet every time, I would get distracted by a man. And end up making stupid decisions. I don't want to do that anymore."

He understood what she was saying. Basically she was blaming men for everything that had gone wrong in her life, and while he wanted to protest that he was different from the men that she had been with, he understood.

"I think it's really big of you to put your kids first. There are a lot of parents who can't do that, can't or won't. And the kids suffer."

"They didn't ask to be brought into this world. They're here because of the stupid decisions I made. And until they're old enough to take care of themselves, and even then... I don't think a mother's job ever ends. I want to be the kind of mother they look back on and are happy that they had, instead of looking at their childhood like a great big mess. Which is how I feel it's been so far."

He felt like he'd already been rejected, and he wanted to just shut up and look away. Not at what she said, because it was all good, but he couldn't help but say, "I would give them a stable home."

She looked down, lightly tracing the arm of her chair. "I know you would. But what if you got sick of me? What if I did something stupid and you got angry? I mean, I know I'm going to."

"So? We all do."

"And then you say you want me out of your house. You want me out of your life. And then the kids get ripped from a home once more, and I have nowhere to go, and I'm staggering around, trying to reorient myself and create a new home. I'm done creating new homes."

"I never started. I only ever wanted to create one." It was true. He thought that he would only be married one time. Planned on it. He planned to choose carefully and make a wise decision.

This was not his plan.

"And you deserve someone that you can create an actual home with, not a big mess like me, who already comes with five kids and is the most unstable person you've ever met."

"I'll leave the decision up to you. I guess I'd ask that you pray about it."

She snorted. "All right. I want to say that God doesn't care who I marry, because He obviously hasn't cared before, but it's pretty easy for me to see that I'm the one who was running away from God and not the other way around. I still... I'm still struck by the deep faith that you obviously have in God. It's...inspiring."

He nodded. "There's a deep faith there. But God's had to work with me a few times. I've...tried to run ahead of Him, and it hasn't worked out well."

"You ran ahead of God? I thought that was just me."

They were getting off the subject, and he was pretty sure that her rejection stood. He wanted to go off somewhere by himself and think about it or get something for his hands to do so his mind could spin without him having to feel the rejection. But they were stuck in the prayer room together, and she was being nice. He couldn't turn away from her and treat her terribly just because she didn't do what he wanted her to.

"When I was younger, I thought I found the right girl." He paused for a second, wondering if he should tell the story of Candace. "I was wrong." There wasn't any point in telling it. Although, the humiliation still made him feel itchy, and he wanted to squirm in his seat.

"There's a story there," she said softly.

"It's old and not any good anyway," he replied, thinking that maybe if she had said yes to his proposal, he would owe her the story. After all, she'd need to know or at least she deserved to know if she were going to be his wife. But since he would just be a friend and probably not a very good one at that, he didn't owe it to her at all.

And he didn't want to dredge up the old feelings and memories.

"All right. I suppose I have some stories in my past that I don't particularly want to share either." Her hand kept moving on the arm of the chair, and then she finally said, "Do you have that letter?"

"It's at home."

"I'd really like to see it. One billion dollars is a lot of money."

Would she marry him for the money? Maybe he should emphasize that more. But there was a part of him that didn't want the money to be the biggest reason she chose him. He wanted her to look at him and see that he was different from the other men that she had been with. To him, it was obvious. Couldn't she see that? That he wasn't going to shack up with some girl, get her pregnant, and then find someone else better and ditch her like she was just so much trash. He wasn't going to get married and then divorce his wife when someone else better came along. He was going to work to provide for his family so that his wife didn't have to worry, didn't have to move in with her gram, didn't have to live in a shack that looked like it should have been condemned ten years ago. Like the one he moved her out of.

Didn't want his kids to look at every man who walked into the house and wonder if that was going to be their new father. Surely she could see that was the kind of man he was.

"It is. We could help a lot of people," he finally said, figuring that if it was the money that got her, maybe she would see who he really was after she had spent some time with him. It wasn't the strategy that he would use except for the nagging feeling that this was the way it was supposed to be.

"And money will make people do weird things." She laughed a little. "Like proposing marriage to a complete stranger."

He was quiet for a moment, looking over her shoulder and out the door at a couple who had just been called back to the ER as they disappeared around the corner.

The waiting room had gotten less crowded and busy and had quieted down.

He pressed his lips together, and then he said, "You mentioned my faith just a moment ago."

"I admire it. I… I guess if I'm going to be a Christian, that's the kind of faith I want. The kind of faith that you obviously have."

"The reason I asked you to marry me is not exactly about the money."

"Really?" She seemed like she couldn't understand how to reconcile how they had been talking about faith, and then he went right into talking about the billion dollars.

"No. Before I got the letter, your gram talked about you a lot. Every time she did, I just had this nagging feeling that God wanted me to do something for you. Something… I didn't know what. I couldn't figure out what. But then, as I thought about it, I just felt like God wanted me to marry you. I know that's weird because we never met," he added hastily when she looked at him in disbelief.

"That's the craziest thing I've ever heard."

"Crazier than someone getting thrown into a den of hungry lions and not getting eaten? Crazier than having the world covered by a flood with one man and his wife and three kids and their spouses surviving? Crazier than a man being crucified on a cross, placed in a tomb, and then resurrected?"

He didn't mean to overwhelm her, but he could tell she was familiar with the Bible stories he referenced, and she got his point as her lips closed and her smile became self-deprecating.

"Okay. I see what you're saying. God does crazy things."

"Yeah. Not all the time. I think most of the time, He works within the bounds of the laws that He set down. But there is one story in the Bible, the story of Hosea."

Her face wrinkled up, and her brows drew down. "I'm not familiar with that one."

"I guess the story isn't very important." He could hardly say that Hosea was commanded to marry a prostitute. He certainly wasn't looking at Tosha as though she were one, and he didn't want her to get the idea that he was.

"God just commanded him to marry someone. Someone that no one would ever think that he would have married, considering that he was a prophet of the Lord. But Hosea obeyed God's command." Eventually Hosea's wife not only bore him children but then left the family and went back to prostitution. He didn't want to depend on that story too much because he absolutely did not want to think about the idea that Tosha might marry him, create a home with him, and then leave. The idea sounded more painful than what he had been through before.

"So you're comparing yourself to an Old Testament prophet?" she asked, and while there was a little bit of mockery in her voice, he could hear her thinking about things too.

"No. I'm not comparing myself to Hosea at all. I'm just saying that sometimes God asks us to do things that we would think were crazy or absolutely wrong, and most of the time, I would say if it goes against the Bible, it's not God telling you to do it. But in this instance, I couldn't get away from it. I would pray, and God would always lead me back to that story. But I didn't know how to reach out to you; we didn't know each other. And then when your gram said she was bringing you here, I figured that it was just the Lord working things out so that I would have the opportunity to see if you might be interested in an old man like me."

She laughed. "You're not that old."

"I'm ten years older than you are."

"You probably are."

She didn't disclose her age, but she really didn't need to. If she was pregnant at sixteen or seventeen, she wasn't more than twenty-three or twenty-four, if that. He was over thirty, so maybe it wasn't ten years, but it was close.

"And then, when your grandma asked me to go help you move, of course I said yes."

"But I don't understand how the letter and the money comes in. I know that has to have affected you. No matter how big your faith is, no matter how deep your convictions, one billion dollars is going to move any man."

"I didn't get the letter until after I had decided that it truly was the Lord telling me I was supposed to marry you. I got the letter, and I realized that that was probably God moving. And then your grandma asked me to help you move. So yeah, I've had the letter for a few weeks and haven't done anything about it. I suppose I'm dragging my feet because... I don't think I want to marry someone I don't know any more than you do."

"It's nice to hear you say that. You don't have the past baggage I do. You haven't sworn off ever getting married again or had relationships the way I have, where I end up with children, no partner to help me raise them, and I've done a lot of things that I know I shouldn't have." She paused for a moment, and then she looked him straight in the eye. "I think God has a better girl for you than me. And I'm not just saying that. If you look at me and what I've done, I don't deserve a man like you. And you deserve someone far better."

"We don't usually get what we deserve." But he wasn't going to stop there. "And I don't deserve anyone better. I think... I think if it's truly God telling me that I'm supposed to marry you, you are the most perfect woman in the world for me."

"No. I'm not perfect for anyone." She shifted in her seat as though the conversation were making her uncomfortable. He actually had been more comfortable in that conversation than he was in the previous where he was asking—it felt like begging—for her to marry him.

Explaining his reasons felt a whole lot safer than asking for someone to just turn him down.

"You can say that if you want to, but I disagree. God made you just as much as He made me. And maybe we made different choices, but that doesn't change who we are at our core, and if we're covered by the blood, then we're children of God, and that makes us equal."

"There is no world in which you and I are equal." She looked at him under her brows, then shook her head and looked away.

"I guess we'll just have to disagree on that."

"We're not going to fight?" she asked, looking at him almost as though she would like to fight.

"No. There is no need to fight. That's no fun."

"You are the first man I've ever heard say that. It seemed like all the other guys I've ever been with, all they want to do is fight. Or argue; they want to win."

"I don't mind winning, that's for sure. I suppose that's a man thing."

"It must be a human thing, because I like to win too. I guess I should say I don't like to lose."

"Excuse me," a voice said, startling them both. He had been so involved in their conversation that he'd almost forgotten that they were even in the hospital. "Are you two here for Mrs. Wells?"

"We are," Tobias said while Tosha nodded beside him.

"She's back from her test, and one of you can go back. It's started to clear out, and perhaps both of you will be able to be back in a few minutes."

"Would you like to go?" He looked at Tosha, who shook her head.

"You go ahead."

He looked at her a bit more, trying to make sure he wasn't doing something that she didn't want him to do. If she wanted to be back with her grandmother, he would certainly let her. As much as he loved the old lady, he wasn't any kind of relation.

"All right. Text me if you need me."

"And you text me if you hear anything."

"I will." He stood and followed the nurse back out of the waiting room and around the corner. Maybe it was just his imagination, but he thought he felt Tosha's eyes on the back of his head the whole time. And he wished that their conversation had ended a little differently. But if it wasn't meant to be, it wasn't meant to be. He'd done what he thought God wanted him to, and after that, it was out of his hands.

Chapter Sixteen

Tosha shifted in her chair. Tobias had gone back about five minutes ago, and she couldn't get their conversation out of her head. He talked about so many things, but the thing she seemed to be stuck on was the fact that he was a good man, the best man who'd ever had even the slightest bit of interest in her, and she turned him down. He had really wanted her to marry him. He hadn't begged her to, but he'd definitely tried to talk her into it, and then he'd gone so far as to say that he thought God wanted them to marry.

Either he really wanted her, or he really believed God wanted him to. She thought the second was true. Still, that made her question everything she thought about God. Maybe God really did convince this good man that he should be with her. That seemed so out of character for what she believed about God, who seemed to be a God of judgment and anger and who put every roadblock in her path He possibly could. But again, that had been her blaming God for her bad choices. It really wasn't His fault that He allowed her to do what she wanted to do, even though she would have appreciated it if He would have stopped her.

But He didn't. He allowed her free will, but that meant that she also had the free will and ability to come back to God.

Lord, I know we haven't talked in a while, unless I was yelling at You, and I'm sorry about that. I don't know what's going on with Tobias. He seemed sure that You're talking to him, and I have a hard time believing it. Would You really send that man to me? Would You really tell him he's supposed to marry me?

And then her vanity took over, and she realized that if God was telling him that he should do it, that meant Tobias really didn't give a flip about her. He was just doing what God wanted.

Sorry, Lord, I want a man who actually wants me for me. Not someone who's just doing what You want him to.

She crossed her arms over her chest as someone sat down in the chair beside her. She recognized the lady who had been sitting a few chairs down.

"Hey. I happened to walk by the prayer room when you were talking to that man, and I heard a bit of your conversation. I hope you don't hold it against me." She continued before Tosha could say whether or not she was going to hold that against her. "I thought that man was asking you to marry him. And I thought you said no."

"Yeah, that's pretty much right," Tosha said, wondering when the woman was going to start talking about the billion dollars. Was it possible she didn't hear that?

"I don't understand why you're telling him no. I didn't hear the whole conversation, but he doesn't seem like the kind of man who would cheat."

"He's not." She could admit that easily. Tobias seemed like the kind of man who would plant his feet and stay there forever. He wasn't going to go flirting with any other girls. He didn't even flirt with her.

"Then I don't understand what your problem is. He's good looking, tall, and he's not fat or bald."

"I guess I wouldn't care if he were fat or bald or tall or good looking, as long as he had good character and integrity."

She resisted the urge to put a hand on her own stomach. After five children, she was hardly the willow-thin girl that she had been back when she was sixteen. She'd put on a few pounds. A few dozen pounds would be more like it.

"Then what's your problem, missy?"

"He doesn't love me." Why did those words come out of her

mouth? She had told Tobias that she had sworn off men. That was the reason she was telling him no. Did she really need him to love her in order for her to say yes?

"A man like that isn't going to tell you that he loves you. He's going to show you. He's going to do things for you. Like open your door, bring home his paycheck, and hand it to you. Play with your kids, and make sure your car is filled up with gas. He's going to be that solid person who's always there for you, no matter what. He's not going to leave you, and he's not going to make googly eyes at some other girl. Who cares if he can't say the words?"

Tosha kept her mouth closed. It never occurred to her that Tobias might have been unable to utter the words "I love you." She had heard about men like that, but in her experience, the men she had been around rattled the words off easily. By the first date even, they might say that they loved her and pledge their undying love and devotion to her. Then two months later, they'd be gone. Or kicking her out.

"He doesn't need to say the words, although you have to admit they're nice." She did like hearing them. There was something about those words that made her heart warm and smile. But she supposed she'd been told the words often enough that rather than hearing the words, she was looking for the actions to back them up. This lady was right. Tobias would be full of those kinds of actions.

"You think I should marry him?"

"I think you should."

"Even though I don't know him? We just met yesterday."

"A man like that is asking you to marry him after you just met yesterday?"

"He told me he thought God wanted him to ask me." She realized he never told her whether or not God had told him whether she would say yes or not. She wondered if he had ever thought of that.

"Really? He thinks the Lord wants you to do it? Girl, you should be running to him."

"Excuse me. Are you Tosha?" A tall man, who looked suspiciously like Tobias, stood in front of her. She looked up, way up, at the man who seemed serious and confident.

"I'm Tosha," she said, standing and holding her hand out. "Who are you?"

It seemed like the man's eyes crinkled just a bit as he looked at her hand, then looked back up at her face. "I'm Ezra, Tobias's older brother. Where did you say he was?"

"I didn't. But he's back with Mrs. Wells. They only let one of us go back at a time."

"I see."

Ezra didn't have time to respond before Tobias walked up and stood between the two of them.

As Tobias greeted his older brother, Tosha turned to say something to the lady who had been sitting beside her, but she was gone.

She looked back at the two men who had shaken hands, although Ezra's eyes seemed to have thunderclouds in them.

"Your gram is sleeping, and I left her without telling her I was leaving. If you want to go back, the nurse said things had cleared out enough that the two of us could be back there together. I need to talk to my brother for a minute first, though." Tobias's words seemed intimate as he bent his head and turned his body toward her, focusing his attention on making sure she was taken care of first.

The words of the lady came back to her. That Tobias was the kind of man who might not say the words "I love you" but would show that with his actions.

He'd already driven the whole way to Sioux City to pick her up and taken her and her children back with him. It was no small thing to make such a long trip with so many kids. He hadn't lost his temper, not even once. Plus, he bought them food, rented them hotel rooms, and did everything in his power to make sure that they were taken care of.

"Thank you. I can walk back."

"You remember how to get there?"

"Yeah. It wasn't hard. But I'll ask a nurse if I need help."

"All right. I'll be right back."

There was something between them, something…intangible but very real, as their eyes met, and she felt herself sway toward him before she forced herself to walk away. Maybe between Tobias thinking the

Lord wanted them together and the strange lady telling her she should, she should give it serious consideration.

Chapter Seventeen

"How was she?" Ezra asked as soon as Tosha walked away.

Tobias pulled his eyes away from Tosha as she rounded the corner, and focused on his brother. He didn't look very happy.

"X-rays have shown her hip is broken. They don't think there are any internal injuries, but they're waiting on a few more test results before they say that conclusively."

"That's good. The broken hip is not good, but the rest of it sounds better than we could have hoped for."

"Yeah. The problem is, they're saying that they'd like for her to go to outpatient therapy, but they're already telling me that her insurance isn't going to pay for it."

"What happens then?"

"Either she goes home, and we take care of her, or someone pays for her therapy."

Ezra's mouth closed, and his jaw jutted out.

Ezra was the only person other than Sawyer Olson and Ford Hansen who knew about the letter.

"Did you ask her to marry you?"

"She said no." Tobias figured he didn't need to sugarcoat it. Ezra had been against him having anything to do with the letter and suggested he throw it away. He said it would cloud his judgment and make him marry someone he shouldn't.

Tobias glanced around the waiting room. The lady who had been sitting beside Tosha when he walked in had left, and Ezra and he were in there by themselves.

"I feel like I am supposed to. I felt like I was supposed to do something to help her since Mrs. Wells started talking about her."

"As long as you're sure it's the Lord telling you."

"I felt like I needed to marry her before I got the letter. The letter was just one more nudge in that direction making me feel like it was God's will for me to do that. But you don't have to worry about it, I told you she said no."

"She's crazy," Ezra muttered, shoving a hand through his hair and taking a few steps before turning around and pacing back, stopping to stand in front of Tobias again.

"You should be thanking her. She might have saved me from making a huge mistake."

"I worry about you." That's all Ezra said, but he didn't need to say more. He was referring to everything that happened before.

"I'm over it."

"I don't know how you ever get over anything like that. It might lead a man to do something crazy so that he didn't have to stick his neck out again over something he really cared about."

"No. That doesn't have anything to do with this." Tobias shook his head, knowing it was true. That wasn't the reason that he had asked Tosha to marry him. Because it was easier.

"You can't deny that asking someone for whom you have no feelings to marry you isn't the same as asking someone whom you're deeply in love with."

"You're a good one to talk. I don't know that you and Alaska had a lot of feelings between the two of you when you guys got married."

"But I knew they could come. And they have. I love her more than life, and she knows it."

"She loves you the same way," Tobias said, crossing his arms over his chest and looking away. That was the kind of love that he wanted. Someone who loved him more than life, someone who felt like they completed his very soul, who knew him on an intimate level and still thought he was the most wonderful man in the world, even though they were well aware of his faults and still thought that anyway. Someone who could respect and admire him, and didn't care about his idiosyncrasies.

That person wasn't Tosha. All she could see was that he was a man and therefore the enemy.

Okay, maybe it wasn't quite that bad, but it felt like it.

"The reason I'm here is because my wife sent me to let you guys know that Tosha's children will be taken care of until Mrs. Wells is better."

"Thank you. I appreciate that."

Ezra put a hand on his shoulder. "I know that the money would make it nice, especially considering that Mrs. Wells would need out-of-pocket expenses paid in order to go to a rehab center, but don't let that lead you into making decisions that are going to ruin the rest of your life. Money can't buy a good marriage. Even one billion dollars. It just can't."

"If you get the right person, the feelings might come." Tobias met Ezra's eyes and knew that Ezra could not deny what he said. After all, he just admitted that the feelings had come between him and Alaska.

"You're right. And if God is telling you to do something, just ignore your older brother, because all I know is I love you and I want to see the best for you, but I can't see any further than that. And I know God loves you and wants the best for you even more, and so... He can see things I can't. Trust Him."

He felt like he had Ezra's stamp of approval as Ezra walked away. He felt like he had God's stamp of approval too. But that didn't matter at all, not as long as Tosha was still saying no.

And he, clumsy and inept as he was around women and burned as he had been, didn't know how to change her mind.

Lord, I'm going to leave that in Your hands. You know women better than I do, since You made them. Good luck.

He didn't roll his eyes as he walked out of the waiting room and down the hall toward Mrs. Well's room and the woman who had just spurned him.

Chapter Eighteen

Twenty-four hours later, Tobias opened the door to her gram's house so Tosha could walk in. Her feet felt like they weighed a hundred pounds each, and she was mentally and physically exhausted.

But she hadn't seen her kids for a full twenty-four hours after moving them to a completely different state and dropping them off with strangers. In a strange house. The whole time she was at the hospital with her gram, she felt guilty for not being with her kids, but the idea of leaving her gram alone in the emergency room all night felt terrible as well.

They hadn't gotten her a room until this morning, and by then, her gram was in a good bit more pain.

Tobias had been by her side the entire time, but he hadn't tried to take over. Which she appreciated. He had given her all the support she needed, and made decisions when she needed him to, but deferred to her as long as she wanted to be in control. He hadn't argued with her or even given her any looks that said that he didn't think she was doing the right thing. Whatever she decided, he was completely behind her.

They had a whispered conversation about whether or not they should allow the hospital to send her gram to rehab. The doctor they talked to said it could happen as early as today. It hadn't, and they'd stayed almost until visiting hours were over.

But now she was back, and Bailey and River ran to her, wrapping their arms around her legs as Joanna and Stonewall stood up from the table where they were eating supper.

"How is your gram?" Joanna said, smiling at the children who had attached themselves to her. Gemmy would have been there begging to be picked up if she hadn't been in a booster seat at the table. As it was, she banged on her tray and said, "Mama! Mama!"

Even Mitchell looked happy to see her.

She gave Joanna the rundown on her gram, which was all good news, except the fact that her insurance wasn't going to pay for any kind of outpatient rehabilitation. She and Tobias had talked about that a little bit during the day, with her asking him how much he thought the rehabilitation would cost. He hadn't had any idea but said they could probably figure on several hundred dollars a day, if not more. He also said he'd try to look it up.

But after that, he hadn't had time, and they had a couple of days at least according to the doctor. The doctor had wanted to give them as much warning as possible, since he knew it was going to be a difficult decision.

"Were the kids good?" she asked, noting that Joanna looked happy, rested, and like she'd just been having an easy day doing something she loved, rather than watching five rambunctious children.

Stonewall seemed just as cool and collected as Joanna, and he also seemed interested in her answer about her gram.

"We had a lot of fun," Joanna said, looking at the kids and then grinning at Stonewall.

"We were able to keep Joanna in line for the most part. I don't think your kids learned too many bad habits from her." Stonewall seemed reluctant to leave the food in front of him, but he stood up and came over to the adults, putting a chummy hand on Joanna's shoulder.

"Don't you mean I was able to keep you from teaching them how to let gas out of both ends at the same time, and you did start giving them a lesson on picking their noses, but I shut that down immediately.

Hopefully no harm done." Joanna's smile was wide, and Tosha couldn't quite figure out whether she was joking or not.

"You can finish eating. You're welcome to stay for a bit if you'd like. We don't want to run you off in the middle of the meal."

It hadn't escaped Tosha's notice that Tobias had been very quiet. In fact, most of the day he'd been quiet. Maybe that was his normal personality. Maybe he'd been talking to her more than he usually spoke at all. Come to think of it, he hadn't talked much in the vehicle while they had been traveling to North Dakota. Maybe he wasn't usually a very talkative person.

But he was definitely a deep thinker, and the things he did say were well-thought-out. She also really appreciated having him beside her, even if he wasn't talking the whole time. He was listening and thinking and gave her some good advice anytime she asked for it.

The kids chattered and soon went back to their seats to finish eating. Joanna dragged two more chairs to the table, squishing Bailey and River together so that Tobias and Tosha could sit down.

Tobias waited for her to take a seat before he sat beside her. Somehow she was acutely aware of his presence and his closeness as well as she chatted with Joanna and Stonewall.

After they were done eating, the kids wanted to take them outside to show them what they had done, but Tosha said that she needed to stay in and clear off the table with Joanna. She wasn't going to let Joanna do it by herself.

Tobias went out, and so did the three older children. He held Gemmy in his hand after Tosha put a coat on her.

"Your kids are so sweet. They just want to be a help. Mitchell was a little bit of a turkey, but in the very best way," Joanna chattered as she cleared off the table.

"Good. I was a little bit worried about them. I dragged them here from Sioux City, and then I just up and left them with strangers. And while you guys seemed really nice to me, sometimes kids are weird."

"I know. Sometimes you just never know what in the world is going to set them off, but everyone was just fine. It probably helps that they have siblings to hang out with. I know when my parents died, that's what kept me going, that and Stonewall. I didn't feel like I was alone, you know?"

"That must have been terrible."

"It was. Devastating. But even though I felt like I had my foundation shaken, I still had my support system in place. A large family is great that way."

"Especially when they're close. If you guys weren't so close, it would be different. Do you really all live on the same ranch together?"

"We do. It's a lot of fun. Although, sometimes we get on each other's nerves, I guess. And as we marry off, some of us are settling down off the ranch, but we work there every day. I do have one sister who might go back to Wyoming."

"That's where you guys are from?"

"Yeah. A little bit different than North Dakota, but there's a lot of wind always, a lot of heat in the summer, and it's almost as cold in the winter." Joanna laughed.

She was so cheerful and infectiously happy that Tosha couldn't help but smile, and somehow being around her made her feel...more positive, like things were going to turn out okay. She wished she could have that kind of happy, always cheerful personality.

Was that a choice? Could she be like that?

She knew that looking at other people and wishing she had what they had was just a recipe for unhappiness.

She finished carrying the plates from the table to the sink and set them down where Joanna had started to run water to wash dishes.

"Can I ask you a question that's a little bit personal?" she said before she had really thought about it. She was curious about Tobias and wanted to pick Joanna's brain. But...would it be too obvious? After all, Tobias was the one who had asked her to marry him. It wasn't like she was digging for information on him because she was interested and he wasn't.

"Sure. I'd love to help you out. Ask away." Joanna rinsed a plate and set it in the drainboard.

"Can you tell me about Tobias? What kind of man is he?"

"Tobias?" Joanna turned to look at her fully, as though wanting to see her face when she answered.

"Yeah. Your brother."

"Well, we grew up pretty close, since we're close in age, and he's awesome. He's quiet, doesn't say a whole lot. But maybe that's because I was around and was chattering all the time. That could be why he could never get a word in edgewise or something."

"So he never talked a lot?"

"Not that I can recall. It's not like he's afraid to talk or anything. He just often waits until he has something worthwhile to say. I guess if I thought about it, he was always a bit of an old man. You know? Just acted older or more mature than everyone else. Except for Ezra who is the oldest, and he was always controlling and in charge."

Joanna lifted her shoulder. "But Tobias was quiet, steady, and if he didn't think something was right or didn't want to do something, you couldn't talk him into it or out of it. Once he made up his mind, he was set, and there are probably things that he still does or doesn't do today because he made up his mind when he was, like, three." Joanna laughed again.

"Really?" Tosha said, trying to picture a little boy who was so serious and set. It wasn't really hard to see Tobias being a serious child.

She wrung out her dishrag and walked over to the table to wipe Phoenix's face off. He was happy sitting in his high chair playing with some crackers, and so she didn't bother to get him down. It would just mean that she'd have to hold him, and that would make everything else she did that much more difficult, to do it with the baby on her hip.

"He did have a pretty hard time when he was a teenager. I mean, I think everyone goes through the teenage years and has a scrape or two and a couple of scars on their psyche to show for it, but... Tobias really got hurt." Her voice kind of trailed off, and Tosha wondered if that was the thing about his old girlfriend that Tobias didn't tell her. It seemed like maybe he was going to, but he didn't.

"Does it have to do with an old girlfriend?" she finally asked when Joanna didn't say anything more but kept washing dishes in the sink.

Tosha looked at the table as she wiped it, but her ears were pricked, listening as hard as she could to what Joanna was going to say.

"It does, but I don't think that it's my story to tell. If Tobias is interested in you, I'm sure that he's going to tell you before you get serious. It...was really hard for him."

"All right." Tosha paused. "He asked me to marry him." Should she have told her? She didn't typically go around telling all of her personal details to everyone she met, but she just really felt like she wanted to talk about this with someone, and Gram hadn't been as alert as she usually was, and she didn't want to burden her with it anyway. Plus, it had taken her a little bit to come to grips with the fact that he actually had asked her to marry him. A complete stranger. It seemed so unbelievable.

"You're kidding?" Joanna had completely stopped washing dishes and turned around, dishwater dripping on the floor.

"I know. Unbelievable, isn't it? I'm hardly the type of girl—"

"No. It's not that. Just... Tobias never does anything on the spur of the moment. I mean, he had to have fallen in love with you at first sight for him to have done that."

"I think it has more to do with him thinking he could help me if we got married." She didn't want to talk about the billion dollars. If Tobias hadn't told his family about it, she didn't want to be the one to spill the beans on that for sure. That was most definitely his story to tell.

"He can help you without marrying you though. And I can't imagine Tobias... You know what, yes, I can. Tobias is very rational. He will definitely make decisions based on what he thinks is the best thing and not necessarily based on his emotions. Which is probably a good thing. When we start to rely too much on our emotions to tell us what we should be doing, we get ourselves into trouble."

Tosha thought about that for a moment. Joanna was right. Every time she depended on her emotions to tell her what to do, she ended up in worse trouble than she'd been in to begin with. Every marriage she entered, every time she moved in with a guy, every baby that she had was because of her emotions getting the best of her.

"I guess no one ever told me that. But I think you're right. Just thinking back over my life for five seconds, I can see about a hundred times where I made decisions based on my emotions and they were foolish, bad decisions."

"See? And Tobias isn't like that. But maybe he's too far the other way. Sometimes you don't know what he's feeling. He's so stoic. And

I'm not sure exactly why. Maybe what he went through when he was younger is part of the reason. He keeps the way he's feeling close to his vest. But he isn't stingy with his advice, and he would help absolutely anyone. Case in point, asking you to marry him. It probably almost has to be something that he thought long and hard about, because I just can't imagine Tobias coming off of that in the spur of the moment, like I said." Joanna had turned back around and was washing dishes again as she spoke casually. "When's the wedding?"

Tosha paused, thinking for a moment. Joanna just assumed that she had said yes. Why? Because Tobias was such a catch? Because Tosha obviously needed someone like Tobias and she would be a fool to turn him down?

"What makes you think I said yes?" she finally asked, too curious to let it go.

Joanna laughed, and Tosha couldn't take offense. "I guess Tobias just seems like a really amazing man. I can't imagine why anyone would turn him down, but I guess if you just met him two days ago, I can totally understand why. After all, you have five kids to consider. He could be a serial killer."

"But he's not."

"No. He's one of the best men you'll ever meet. If not the very best. I have six brothers, so I don't know that I can say for sure that he is the absolute best man, but he's definitely tied with the rest of them. He's... honest and has character and integrity, and saying yes would be the best decision of your life."

Joanna chuckled as she reached for another dish.

"My opinion is biased. I admit. Although, if I had to choose a brother to help me in a pinch, Tobias and Ezra would be at the top of the list. Not that I don't love my other brothers, but those two are the best thinkers and the ones that will give me a hand no matter what. Tobias even more than Ezra will sacrifice whatever necessary to take care of anyone he considers his."

Chapter Nineteen

Did Tosha need to talk about it anymore? Was that all she needed to hear? If she had the possibility of having a man who would sacrifice anything in order to protect her and her children, wouldn't she be one hundred different kinds of fool to turn that down? So what if he didn't love her. If he was loyal to her, if he protected and provided for her, if he kept his word and stayed true, what more could she ask for?

Was she settling? She didn't feel like she was settling. In fact, she felt like she was reaching for the sun, moon, stars, and the entire solar system all wrapped up in one, since getting Tobias would be more than she ever dreamed of or could possibly have hoped for.

She didn't have a chance to ask Joanna any more questions because just as Joanna pulled the drain out of the sink, the door opened and her children came rushing back in along with Tobias and Stonewall.

Stonewall and Joanna left shortly afterward, and by the time Tosha figured out where the kids' clothes were, got them baths, and got their jammies on and read them several stories, it was time for bed.

By that time, she was wondering something else. If her grandma went to rehab, and they ended up having to sell the farm to pay for her care, Tosha would again be out of a place to live.

The idea of not having a place to live, yet again, pulled her stomach tight in a painfully uncomfortable way. She thought coming to her gram's would give her the security that she desperately wanted, but her gram's injury and the decisions that she was going to have to make could make it so that her life was even more unstable than what it had been before. After all, living in Sioux City, she could at least get a job somewhere. Here, she was so far away from anything that it would be difficult to get any kind of work. And then, in the winter, she would have the added difficulty of trying to drive to her job and deal with her children and her gram and whoever was watching them.

The doctor had warned them that if her gram didn't go to a rehab center, she most likely wouldn't get the therapy she needed and could possibly be bedridden for the rest of her life. Tosha had figured that sending her to rehab would be the very best decision for her grandma. The problem was, the only way to pay for it was to sell the farm. And even then, she wasn't sure that she would have enough in order to completely cover the bill. What then? If she had her gram's rehab on top of no job and no place to stay, she'd be in a terrible position. Plus, she would have her gram to take care of as well.

And there were no guarantees that her gram would ever walk again. That's what the doctor had told them.

"It was a big day. Are you ready for bed?"

Tobias had been helping her by bringing some things in from the car, getting drinks for the kids, and tucking them into bed. He even read a chapter from their book to Mitchell and Bailey.

She didn't understand why he was giving her a hand unless it was to help butter her up. But he didn't seem like he was trying to do that. He definitely wasn't flirting now. He was just asking her if she was ready for bed.

"Did you ever get a chance to research how much it cost at the rehabilitation hospital?"

"The website said it was between seven and eleven hundred dollars a day, depending on the care."

"Wow. That was even more than I was expecting."

"Yeah. I'm sorry I didn't look that up earlier, and I didn't figure that was something you wanted to talk about in front of the children. Not that they would understand it all."

"Yeah. I guess me being worried about it in front of them doesn't help anyone."

"There's no need to worry about it. Just pray."

He made it sound so easy. She wanted to smack him. Life wasn't as easy as what he made it out to be. Life was hard. It was a struggle. It knocked you down then kicked you for good measure and then laughed about it.

But her new way of thinking was to remind herself that she had made all the bad decisions that had led to her being knocked down and kicked by life. If she started making better decisions, even though they were hard decisions at the time, she might have different outcomes.

She had to take responsibility for her life. She couldn't sit around blaming everyone else. Even God. Although that was a little bit harder, because God could have changed things. Some people made really terrible decisions and ended up sitting on top of the world despite them.

"You're thinking hard?" Tobias asked, leaning against the bathroom doorjamb. He had a hand on the railing, as though he were headed back downstairs but was waiting on her to make a decision as to whether she was going to go down or stay up.

"Why is it that some people make really bad decisions and nothing bad ever seems to happen because of it?"

"You reap what you sow. Some crops take longer to harvest than others, but there's always a harvest, and you always get what you sow."

"That doesn't answer my question."

"Maybe their lives aren't as good as what they look. Maybe things are worse than what they seem. Maybe you don't see how things are not turning out well for them."

She supposed that could be true. Some of the women she knew who had been even more promiscuous than she might have hidden STDs that no one knew about. Maybe they had abortions instead of having their children and carrying their children around like they were showcasing their poor decisions.

"I suppose you could be right. It just seems like…I've been punished for every single wrong thing I've ever done, am still being punished, even though I want to turn my life around. How do you turn your life around when bad things just keep piling up on you so much that you don't even feel like you could ever crawl out from underneath them?"

"You accept the proposal from the guy who offered to marry you."

Her eyes snapped to his where she found humor and a smile lurking about his lips. She huffed out a laugh. "That was nice. Very nice. Smooth. Great move."

"Thanks. I was waiting for the right opening." He straightened, shifting, before leaning a hip against the banister and wrapping a hand around his neck. "I'm kidding. I really wasn't looking for an opening to push. But if we got married, we get the money, your gram will be taken care of, the farm's taken care of, I have some things that I need to take care of with my family, and that could go away as well. We...would not have financial difficulty. But there will be some other things we have to work through, and I'm not going to be so naïve as to try to pretend that there won't be problems that we have to walk through."

"That's true. There definitely would be some things we would need to deal with."

It was on the tip of her tongue to ask about what Joanna had meant when she had said that one of his previous girlfriends had put him through an extremely difficult time. And that he had probably learned from those things and perhaps wasn't as effusive with his emotions as a result. But did it matter?

"Are you still in love with someone else?"

That mattered. Even though she figured that he probably would be true to her no matter what. If he were half the man everyone seemed to think he was.

"No." He didn't elaborate.

"Joanna said that there was a girlfriend and that perhaps some of your personality was shaped by some of the things that happened to you, and she insinuated that it was not good."

"She's right."

"If I agree to marry you, should I know about that?"

Dark had already fallen outside, and while there was still light on in the bathroom that shone down the hall that she would probably leave on all night just in case any of her children got up and needed to go to the restroom, his face was still in shadows, and she couldn't read his expression as he seemed to stare down at her.

"I wouldn't say that you need to know about it, but I definitely want to tell you."

"If the offer is still open, I accept."

There. That was a decision made. And surprisingly, she felt lighter, easier, and happier after the words were out of her mouth. It wasn't nearly as hard as what she thought it was going to be and not nearly as stressful. Maybe it was the idea that she knew exactly what kind of man Tobias was. Or maybe it was because the money would definitely ease some of her problems. Although like she had just told Tobias, she knew there were still going to be problems. But didn't it make sense to take care of the problems that she was able to take care of?

She kinda figured it did.

"Just like that? What made you change your mind?" Tobias did not sound happy. He also didn't sound angry or upset. He just didn't sound like a man who just got what he wanted.

"Was the offer still open?"

"It is. I'm glad you've accepted. But I was just wondering what made you change your mind?"

"I can see from being around you that you're an honest and upright man. I guess the idea that you have to be in love in order to get married is so ingrained in our culture that it took me a little bit to realize that maybe I don't. Maybe I don't have to have the gushy feelings and the infatuation and to date for three years before I'm sure that I'm with the one who's going to be compatible with me and that we're going to stay in love for the rest of our lives. I don't think that's the goal. Staying in love. The goal is just to stay. Through hard times and good times and bad times and everything in between. To work together. To build a life. I guess the more I thought about it, the more I knew that I could do that with you, and you aren't going to tear down everything I build and walk away like everyone else I know."

"Thank you, I guess."

"But I would like to know about that ex-girlfriend."

"I'm not asking you about any of your exes."

He had a good point. She didn't really want to tell him anything, although she would tell him anything he asked.

"If you ask, I will answer."

"No secrets?"

Her eyes narrowed. She hadn't known any man to not keep secrets from her. That seemed almost too good to be true that he was actually going to be honest and upfront. But she couldn't expect it out of him if she wasn't willing to give it herself.

"No secrets."

"You want to go downstairs and sit down?"

"Is the story that long?"

"Not necessarily. It's just uncomfortable, and I'd rather be a little bit more comfortable where I'm sitting when I tell the uncomfortable story."

"All right. You want me to make coffee or tea or something?"

"No thanks. But I'll wait while you make it for yourself," he said, waiting for her to walk down the stairs before he followed her.

"I don't need anything. I... I'm a little bit concerned about Gram, but if we really do this and we get the money, I won't have to worry about paying for anything, and that will be a huge burden lifted off. We can get her the very best care possible."

"Sometimes even with the best, things don't work out the way we want them to."

"You're right about that. But if things don't work out, it won't be because we didn't try."

"True."

They walked into the living room, with Tobias switching on a table lamp, but not the big overhead light, and waiting for her to take a seat before he sat down on the loveseat across from the couch.

He did not sit back but rather rested his forearms on his knees and clasped his hands together between them. That seemed to be his default position.

Tosha got the feeling that maybe she shouldn't have asked, and even more than that, maybe she didn't want to know what he was about to share.

Chapter Twenty

Tobias tried to focus on not twisting his hands together. He really didn't want to talk about this tonight, or any night for that matter. But Tosha had just agreed to accept his proposal.

It was funny, because he'd almost talked himself into the fact that he had done what God wanted him to do, and his rejection had been God's plan all along. Probably like Abraham taking Isaac and being willing to sacrifice his son on the altar, and God stayed his hand at the last moment and saved Isaac's life.

Tobias did what God wanted him to do, but God wasn't going to actually make him go through with the marriage to Tosha. Not that a marriage to her was onerous. Although, she wasn't the kind of woman Tobias would have looked twice at or even been interested in had he been looking for a woman to get married to.

But he had quit looking years ago. And now he was about to tell Tosha about Candace.

"If this is too painful, you don't have to do it. I just got the feeling from Joanna that it was a pretty important chapter in your life and that I will be able to understand you a little bit better if we talked about it or I at least knew."

"You're going to be my wife, you should know as much about me as everyone else does. More, actually." He believed that. A wife deserved a special place in a man's life. A place of honor and respect, a place that no other woman was offered. She would be treated the way he treated no other woman. She would get his smiles and his laughter and his flirtations, and she would be the one he spent his time with and the one he thought about when he wasn't with her. Forsaking all others. Wasn't that in the wedding vows? Wasn't that what that meant? That he wasn't going to be interested in anyone else for anything.

But he was getting ahead of himself. He had a story to get to first.

"I like that. I can get on board with it."

"So when I was about twenty-two or twenty-three, after I graduated from college, I met a girl."

She was quiet, listening. Leaning back on the couch, her hands in her lap. She looked relaxed and calm, but attentive.

"Candace was...exactly what I was looking for. She was active in her church, a true Christian, with a heart for Jesus. She was pretty and fun, and somehow she was interested in me too."

"Somehow? Tobias, you're not just attractive, you're compelling."

He wasn't sure what compelling meant, but it didn't seem to make anyone feel like they needed to fall in front of him and declare their undying love, and it just didn't seem to be a compliment. Regardless, he continued.

"She and I started courting. Not dating. We were never alone. We were always with my family or hers. At first, everything was okay, but after a few months, there was something going on that I couldn't quite put my finger on. It turned out, not to spoil the story, that she was seeing someone behind my back. Someone who was magnetic and attractive and exciting. Maybe the most exciting man she'd ever met. But he was also into drugs and some really bad things."

He could feel the tension radiating through his body. He would have done anything for Candace. He wanted to marry her. They had been talking about it, and at first, she had been really interested, but the more involved she got with this guy that he didn't know about at the time, the less interested she was in him, and the more she put him off.

"She didn't break things off with me because she wanted to keep up appearances. Her parents would never have approved of the other guy. So I was her cover."

"She was using you."

He nodded. The pain still sliced down through his torso. "Not at first, but that's how it ended."

He swallowed. His mouth was dry, and he wished he would have accepted the offer of coffee. Or water or something.

"So anyway, I'm sure you can see where this is going. She got pregnant. The dude, when he found out, split. He didn't hang around at all, which devastated Candace."

"I would have married her. I would have made everything right. I still wanted to. But... She didn't want me. She came to my house and asked to see me. She confessed to me what had happened, that she had been intimate with this guy and that now she was pregnant. And that he was the father."

He pulled in a breath through his nose. "I was devastated. Of course. I fancied myself in love with her. I thought we were spending the rest of our lives together. I didn't understand how she could have done this, and was betrayed and hurt and angry all at once. But I still would have married her, taken her baby as mine, but she didn't want me."

"She didn't?"

He shook his head no. "She told me she was going to go after that guy. That she wasn't going to tell her parents, but she was just going to leave. She knew if her parents found out, they would insist on a wedding between the two of us, and she made me promise that I would not marry her."

"Did you promise?"

"I did. I couldn't tell her no. Even though she hurt me and I was reeling from her information, I couldn't deny her that. So I promised that I would not marry her, that I would not allow her parents to make us marry."

He hadn't wanted to. He had wanted to marry her anyway and had suggested they do it, over and over, but she absolutely refused. He took another breath. It had been devastating to have Candace break up with him, but the worst part had been what came after. "She wasn't done talking to me when her parents showed up. Apparently her mother had found the pregnancy test in the garbage can, put two and two together and got five, because they thought I was the dad."

"They really didn't know about the other guy?"

He shook his head no.

They hadn't had a clue. Not even a smidgen of an idea.

"Her dad got out of the car and stormed the porch. I can't believe that my siblings weren't out, they always came out when anyone came, but they were inside having a game night, and I think things were pretty loud. Regardless, her dad came up the porch, and I know that the shotgun is a cliché, but he was holding one, and he told me that I was going to marry his daughter."

Tosha gasped.

That was how he felt. After all, he'd just given his word that he wouldn't, and there was a man with a gun standing in front of him demanding he did.

"What did you do?" Tosha asked, her hand over her mouth, her other hand on her heart.

"I told him, 'No, sir, I won't.'" A ghost of a smile passed over his face. "With the wisdom of years, I probably could have chosen words that would have gone over better, but I felt like I needed to be clear, or I would get pushed into something I wanted, but Candace didn't. And I was not going to make her do something that she didn't want to do. And I wasn't going to go against my word."

"Did you tell him that you had just given your word to Candace that you wouldn't marry her?"

"Also promised that I wouldn't tell anyone who the father was."

"You didn't."

"It didn't occur to me the assumptions that the entire town was going to make. I thought Candace would tell the truth. I thought she would come clean when she saw what was happening to me."

"She didn't?"

He sat still for a moment, thinking about it. He couldn't believe that someone who had claimed to love him, who he had loved with so much ardor and so much fierceness, could have done what she had done. Everything in his young soul had been set on Candace. He had thought she hung the moon and the stars and would be the center of his universe for the rest of his life. And yet, she couldn't even open her mouth to come to his defense.

"No. She never did. She let her dad stand there and demand that I marry her, and she allowed me to say that I wouldn't, without being able to deny that I was the father. Even though her dad was waving a shotgun around in my face, and I wasn't entirely sure he wasn't going to use it. Thankfully, the shouting finally got through to my siblings, and Ezra and Roland and Stonewall, along with my other brothers, came out on the porch, and things started to feel a little bit more fair, because I knew Ezra always had a gun slipped in the back of his waistband. I might get shot, but Ezra would make sure no one else did."

"All right. That's not exactly reassuring," Tosha said, and there was sarcasm in her voice clearly.

"No. But at the time, it did seem that way. Anyway, he grabbed his daughter, and they went home, and by the next morning, the entire town knew that I had gotten his daughter pregnant and refused to marry her."

"Did Candace go find her boyfriend?"

"No. She hung herself."

There was silence in the room. Tobias knew he probably should have said those words a little bit more carefully. Broken it to Tosha a little bit more gently. But that's what happened. And that's how he found out.

"And the entire town blamed you."

"They did."

It had been terrible. He hadn't been expecting that at all. Not Candace killing herself, not the fact that she wouldn't tell anyone who the father was and would allow everyone to think it was him.

"And you had promised you wouldn't say who the father was."

"I know. Was that a promise that I didn't have to keep after she died? I couldn't figure it out. And I couldn't talk to anyone about it without saying what the promise was. I wanted to talk to Ezra. I wanted to tell him what was going on. But I had made promises I couldn't break, especially now that Candace was gone. And... I wrestled with it for a while, but eventually I just let go and let it be what it was."

"Which was the entire town blaming you."

"I wasn't shunned, but I might as well have been. Mothers pulled their daughters away from me as I walked by, no one would talk to me, everyone thought I was terrible, had no values and no morals and no character. And to be honest, I blame myself some for Candace's death. What if I had handled things differently? What if I had refused to promise to not marry her? What if I had begged her to marry me? What if I had told her that I still loved her no matter what she did? I mean, I was hurt, and I suppose when someone is hurt, the thing that they want to do is hurt whoever it was who hurt them, but I could have handled it better, and then maybe she'd still be alive."

"You two would be married." Tosha's voice was flat, almost as though she were bitter or upset.

"Then I guess I wouldn't be here talking to you."

"That doesn't make me happy. Although, what you went through breaks my heart."

He didn't doubt it did. She had sincere reactions to the story, and it was obvious that she felt for him.

"Do you still love her?" Tosha's words were soft, and they sounded insecure, like she truly wondered.

"No. I suppose the blinders fell off my eyes when she told me she was pregnant by that other guy. I had had her up on a pedestal. I was blinded by my emotions. I allowed them to make the decisions for me, and I courted her, even though I knew that she wasn't as into me as I was into her. I thought given time, she'd fall just as hard as I did. I was sure she was the one for me, even though I didn't really talk to the Lord about it. Again, it was all based on my emotions."

"And that's why you're so against emotions dictating decisions."

"I suppose."

He allowed the silence to stretch between them. Now that the story was out, and he didn't have to tell it anymore, he leaned back, putting an ankle on his knee and leaning his head back, looking at the ceiling. He'd sat in this room dozens of times with Mrs. Wells as they chatted, drank coffee, and took a break from the outside cold to warm up and have a bit of companionship. He couldn't believe the woman had fallen and was in the hospital, and he was sitting here with her granddaughter.

He had thought about her granddaughter and his plans for her, but he hadn't thought that by asking her to marry him, he was going to have to dredge up all the terrible feelings from his past.

Maybe someday, he'd be able to talk about it without the feelings coming back. People judging him based on what they thought to be true, but they were dead wrong. Treating him badly because of it even though they had never seen any sign of him being the person that they heard he was. How could they believe those things about him? How could they have painted his character such a terrible color and not allowed him to use his actions to defend himself since he couldn't use his words.

Somehow, he wasn't sure how, but Ezra had learned the truth. Maybe through the grapevine, with the dad bragging that the girl he'd knocked up had taken care of the problem for him so he didn't have to. Tobias had never asked Ezra where exactly he figured it out, but his siblings, while disappointed, had always believed the best about him. And then, when they knew the truth, they had taken the liberty of spreading it around town. But by then, it was too late, and people believed what they wanted to. There were still people in their hometown of Wyoming who believed the worst about him.

But his family always had a spotless reputation, and with time, it had faded, until they had moved to North Dakota to start over after their parents died.

"I hadn't realized how late it was. If you don't mind, I think I'd like to go to bed," Tosha said, rising from the couch.

He stood as well, although he had no desire to go upstairs right now. There were too many emotions whirling through him.

"Think I'm going to take a walk. I'll be in and make sure everything's locked down."

"Thanks," she said, slipping out of the room without looking at him again.

He'd told the story as straightforward as he could, trying not to make himself look any better than he did but definitely not making himself look any worse, either. That was probably an instinct that was ingrained in a human being, to try to make oneself look as good as they could. Fine, maybe he hadn't been successful, or maybe something else was bothering her. He really wasn't sure. But a walk would definitely clear his head, and so he stood up, put his coat on, and walked outside into the dark North Dakota night.

Chapter Twenty-One

Tosha lay in bed staring at the ceiling. She couldn't believe the story Tobias had told her. How terrible to have the woman that he thought he was going to spend the rest of his life with sleep with another man and then hang herself. And then to have all that made so much worse by having the entire town blame him. And make it seem like it was all his fault. And for him to not be able to exonerate himself by telling the truth.

That wasn't really what bothered her, although it made her feel terrible for Tobias. The thing that bothered her was the fact that Tobias obviously was capable of deep, deep feelings. After all, he loved Candace with his entire heart and soul, as he had said. He admitted it. He didn't have a problem telling her how much he loved Candace. So, obviously he was capable of love. Of feeling it and talking about it. That made the fact that he did not love Tosha even harder.

And yet she had agreed to marry him. She shouldn't have, now that she thought about it in hindsight. She should have asked for him to tell the story first, and then she would have known he could never love her and be sure that he didn't love her now. No matter what other people said. And his actions might say that he loved her, but to know that he was capable of saying the words, feeling the feeling, and just didn't, made her feel less than.

But was it worth it to cater to her feelings? Because if she did, a lot of people were going to suffer. Her gram for one, her children, her, and whatever Tobias wanted to use the money for. He said there were things with his family that he needed it for. And Joanna was the sweetest girl in the entire world. How could Tosha decide to go to Tobias and tell him that she changed her mind and didn't want to marry him after all? Knowing that would hurt all of those people, plus more?

She just couldn't. So that left her with one choice. To agree to continue to go through with the marriage.

They hadn't talked about when the wedding would happen, but it had to be soon. He said he had a month, and he'd already had the letter for over three weeks. She just had a couple of days. If that.

The next idea that came into her brain almost made her sit straight up in bed.

Tomorrow this time, she could be married.

She hadn't been nervous at all for her first two weddings. Each time, she'd been sure she was with the person that she would be spending the rest of her life with. But she had been dead wrong. Now, Tobias was not the kind of man to leave, and yet she was scared he would and nervous as all get-out.

Maybe she was just the backward kind of person, the kind of person who fell in love with men she shouldn't, and married those with unsteady character who could lie to people without blinking an eye, and was nervous about agreeing to marry a man who would be steady and there for her for the rest of her life.

It was into the wee hours of the morning before she fell into a fitful sleep, and she woke up feeling like she hadn't slept at all.

She got out of bed anyway, since it was always nice to beat the kids up and get a few things done before they started to come downstairs.

To her surprise when she came down, Tobias was already leaning against the counter, his hands wrapped around a cup of coffee.

"You're up already?" she asked softly.

"Up, fed the stock, and back in again getting my hands warm. I figured I would cook breakfast when the kids got up, but I wasn't sure what time that would be."

"Anytime now. I slept in a little bit more than I usually do, because... I guess I'm nervous. We didn't really hash out any details about our wedding."

"You didn't seem very happy with me before you went to bed."

He'd noticed. She wasn't used to having a man in her life who actually noticed her moods and was so in tune with the things that she was feeling. To her, having someone who knew how she was feeling showed that the person cared about her. But did that mean Tobias cared? Or did it mean that he was just good at reading people?

Part of her believed the second, since the first was so hard for her to wrap her mind around.

They barely knew each other. How could he care?

But then she remembered how he felt whenever her gram had talked about her. Like he wanted to do something to help her. He cared about her before he even knew her.

"Was it something I said?" he finally said when she didn't say anything more.

She brought her mind back to the present. He had mentioned that she wasn't very happy with him before she went to bed. It was on the tip of her tongue to lie, to say something flippant, but... He had been so deep and honest with her last night that she felt like doing anything less was not holding up her end of the bargain and meeting his standards.

"I guess... I guess there's a little bit of feminine vanity in me that's offended."

"Offended?" His brows raised, but he seemed curious more than derisive. She had been prepared for the derision. She was getting used to the curiosity.

"Not angry or offended, just... If we're going to get married, I... I guess I get that you don't love me. But I suppose it hurts a little—the idea that you don't when you really loved Candace. I suppose my feminine vanity is hurt because I don't want to marry someone who was in love with someone else or still is."

"I definitely am not. Whether I was or not at the time, I've often wondered. After all, I told you, it was all feelings."

"There's nothing wrong with feelings. Sometimes we need to feel our feelings."

"You saw what happened when I felt my feelings. It ended up being a mess."

"If you're married, it's okay to feel your feelings."

"All right. When we're married, I will feel my feelings."

How did this turn into a joke? But he was smiling and she was laughing, and she wasn't quite sure what all that meant. Still, she appreciated the fact that he had at least agreed, and from the story that he told last night, the one thing that she knew that she could depend on was that Tobias would keep his word. That was obvious. Maybe that was exactly what he intended for her to learn from that story, but it was her biggest takeaway, other than the fact that he was able to feel love.

"So you're still wanting to get married?"

"I am. Are you?" She lifted her brows in challenge. She didn't want to be the only one in this crazy relationship. It felt so weird, so different than what she had known before. Even though she'd been married twice, this time made everything feel new since it was so different.

"Of course. I'm not going to change my mind."

"Joanna told me that there were probably things you had made your mind up about when you were three years old that you would absolutely still refuse to change it on."

He huffed out a laugh at that. "Joanna is dramatic. Don't pay any attention to her."

"So it's not true?"

"It might be a little bit true," he said, and there was that elusive smile again.

Her eyes caught on it and held, and he quit laughing, and across the kitchen, something seemed to stir between them. Something warm and sweet. Maybe he would never be madly in love with her, but maybe he would at least feel affection for her. The idea wasn't terrible.

"So are we getting married today?" she asked, trying to sound nonchalant. After all, a few days ago, she didn't even know that Tobias existed, and now, she might be getting married to him.

"I think it's a good idea. You asked for the letter, and I got it out and set it on the counter there for you to read. I'm pretty sure the date on it is October 30th. So we have three more days."

"All right. I can read it, but I'll take your word for it too. I'm free all three days, other than the kids."

"My family will help with them. God knows I've babysat my nieces and nephews often enough, everybody owes me."

"Everybody who's married with children," she said.

"True, but I'm sure I'm going to be watching more children, so even the ones that aren't married with children, like Joanna, can give us a hand."

"I don't want your family to hate me."

"They're not going to hate you. They're going to love you because you're mine."

She was his. She hadn't realized how those words would affect her. None of her other husbands talked that way, other than in a mean, possessive, they weren't going to allow her to do anything kind of way. But the way Tobias said it made her feel protected and loved.

There was that word again. The L word. The word she wasn't supposed to ever expect Tobias to say to her.

"If you say so, I'll talk to the pastor and see what he says. He's probably going to want to talk to us a little bit before he marries us, but I know that he'll be okay with us."

"Talk to us about what?"

"Usually he likes to do a little bit of marriage counseling before the nuptials. I learned that through my siblings who got married. I think it's probably a good idea. That way, people know what they should expect. But more than that, the Bible has a lot to say about how husbands and wives should treat each other, and following the Bible is the best roadmap to a happy life."

"Why is that?" she asked, realizing that maybe talking to the Lord for the first time in a long time, just a couple days ago, was the start of a new relationship with Him for her.

"God made us, and God wrote the Bible. It's like our owner's manual. The only thing is, so many of us don't bother to read or follow it. We certainly would never do that with an appliance or anything else that we bought. Yet we do it with ourselves, rather easily."

"Maybe that's because most people don't believe that God actually created us but that we evolved."

"Maybe we choose to believe a lie because we don't want the hardship of knowing the truth."

"Hardship?"

"If the truth is that God made us, then we're bound to follow the Bible, because it's His Word. But if we refuse to believe that truth, then we don't have any parameters that we have to follow, and we can do whatever we want, because nothing is wrong."

"If nothing is wrong, everything is right, even murder." Even she could see that.

"Bingo. Once you have no rules in place, anything goes. Or else society makes the rules, and those rules change as society changes. But then, what kind of rules are those? They're just shifting sands."

She agreed with him, although she'd never thought it out to its logical conclusion before. But if there was no God, then there was no good and no evil. Everything was neutral. Including murder, molestation, even the worst murders in history, where millions of people died, were not good or bad, just neutral, because without God there was no good or bad.

She felt like her eyes had been opened a little, and she shook her head. That seemed to be the effect that Tobias had on her. She thought of things that she hadn't thought of before.

It was good to be with someone who helped her become a better person than she thought she could be. Had she ever been with a man who made her better? She couldn't think of a time. But with that thought came another: did she make him better?

It seemed unfair to him to be with someone who pulled him down, rather than someone who lifted him up. She shouldn't have benefits he didn't get. Even though they'd agreed that life wasn't fair.

"I think I hear the kids stirring," she said, tilting her head and listening. "When one is up, usually they all end up getting up."

"All right. We have all the ingredients for bacon gouda egg bites that my mom always made. They're easy and kid friendly. Then I'll see what's going on with the pastor. We'll want to enroll them in school unless—"

"Unless?" she asked when he didn't finish.

"Unless you wanted to do something else with them. I guess."

"Like what?"

"My parents homeschooled us, but it's a lot of work, and I wouldn't ask you to make that commitment. I just didn't want you to think that your only choice was public school."

"Thank you for letting me know. I... I never thought about homeschooling. I think for now, we'll enroll them, and I guess we'll play it by ear after that."

Homeschooling? He'd been homeschooled? Was that why he was so weird?

She didn't necessarily mean weird in a bad way, just weird in the kind of way that he was different from anyone she'd ever known.

If that was what homeschooling did, maybe she was interested in it for her children. After all, she was definitely benefiting from someone else's sacrifice. Why wouldn't she want her kids and their eventual spouses to benefit from hers?

Chapter Twenty-Two

Stonewall watched Tobias and Tosha exchange vows. Less than a week ago, they'd never even met, today they were pledging their lives to each other. The pastor had done premarital counseling with them earlier in the day, but to get married to someone he barely knew was crazy.

Beside him, Joanna sniffed and dabbed at her eyes.

He pulled the tissue that he'd brought for her out of his pocket and handed it over. She always cried at weddings.

"Thank you," she whispered softly, giving him a watery smile.

He gave her a lopsided grin. He knew her better than he knew himself and couldn't imagine being here without her. Or having something happen in her family that he wasn't invited to.

His family was exactly the opposite, although his mother had been clamoring for him to visit. He had been warned by his sister why his mother wanted him, and after the vows had been exchanged and after Joanna and he had stood behind the table laden with food helping to serve it to the small group of people who had attended the wedding, he managed to get Joanna into a quiet corner so he could talk to her.

"You've been awfully quiet. What's going on?" Joanna said in her usual blunt way. She didn't talk that way with everyone, just her brothers and him. He was special, and he appreciated it. But she had a special place in his life, too. Best friend, confidant, person who went with him everywhere. He wasn't sure what to label her.

"My mom keeps calling me."

"Just tell her no. Although, you know it's been a couple of years since you've seen her. You probably should go home and let her lay eyes on you, so she knows I haven't killed you like she always suspected I would."

"I always thought it was kind of funny how she thought you'd murder me in my sleep. She warned me from you, which was kind of funny because of all the girls I knew, you were the one least likely to murder me."

"I've got you buffaloed. Good. You'll be unsuspecting whenever I finally do stab that knife between your fifth rib or whatever it is? What's that Bible story again?"

"When Joab killed Abner?"

"Yeah, that one."

"But I know you're kidding. Although, that's really nothing to kid about as my mom would say."

"Yes, I know I should be more respectful of your mom, but she's hated me all my life. I don't understand that. Do you?"

"You took her little boy away."

"Well, I can understand her being upset about that. Because I did, except you followed me willingly, and I just went with my family, so I don't know why she'd be upset about that."

She was referring to the fact that when her family moved from Wyoming to North Dakota, he went with them. He always felt more a part of Joanna's family than he did of his own, but Joanna was more than a sibling too. He wasn't quite sure how to explain her.

"The problem is, she's got some girl that she wants to introduce me to and throw at me. And... I just am not interested. I definitely don't want to go home for that, especially if she's not even going to talk to me but is going to constantly be throwing me with this woman she thinks I should be with."

"Have you met her? Do you know anything about her? Maybe she'd be perfect for you. After all, your mom might be annoying, but she loves you."

"Sometimes. Sometimes it seems like she doesn't."

"All right. I'll give you that. Sometimes she can be a little bit weird."

"So can you."

"But you love my kind of weird. Her kind of weird is...creepy."

"You called my mom weird and creepy. I think I should be upset with you."

"Okay. I love your mom. You know I do, but she bothers you, and that bothers me."

"It bothers me too. But I don't know what to do about it. And I don't know what to say to her. She's been blowing up my phone, texting every hour, asking if I'm coming."

"Did you try saying no?"

"I did. But she ignored me and gave me a guilt trip for not being there for the last two years, which you just pointed out was true. What am I supposed to say to that?"

"That you're busy here and you can't pull yourself away from the ranch." Joanna bit her lip. He loved that about her, that she loved his mom, even though his mom had never been kind to her. Joanna had always tried to be kind. But his mom was firm in her dislike.

Stonewall was pretty sure it was because his mom was jealous of Joanna. But he didn't know what to do about that. Joanna was like a sister to him, and he wasn't going to give her up just because his mom didn't like her. Because it was true, Joanna was the best thing that ever happened to him. Better than any other woman he'd ever met. Any other man for that matter too. Although her brothers were really awesome, Joanna was just...special.

"You know, maybe you really should just go home to see your mom. Could you be firm about not wanting to see the girl that she wants you to? Although, maybe you should," she said again.

"What? Are you throwing girls at me too?"

"No. I'm just saying to keep your eyes open. I don't want you to miss someone just because of where she lives."

"Unless she's willing to move to North Dakota, which I highly doubt, I'm not interested. Because I'm not leaving the ranch. You guys need help."

Joanna didn't argue with him, and there really was no point for her to do that. They all knew that they had made the decision to pay for Erin's hospital bill, which was Tillman and his wife's daughter. Tillman was Joanna's brother. But the hospital bill had taken all the rest of their savings, and they were pretty much in desperate straits.

"She's your mom."

"I never understood why you were so nice to her when she hates you."

"I can't help it that she hates me. And I guess I kind of understand. I wouldn't want someone taking you away from me either, so it makes sense to me that she would be so unkind. Not that it makes it any easier."

"I appreciate you being big about it. I guess I'll have to go home... It would be nice if I could do it and somehow not have to deal with whoever it is that she's going to be trying to match me up with."

"Just take a fiancée home with you. Then your mom will leave you alone."

"That sounds easy." He laughed. "Where am I going to get a fiancée? Do you hire them online?"

"I actually think you probably can. I read all kinds of romance novels where people go home for a wedding and they have to hire a date, and there seems to be plenty of places for those people to find one."

"You know romance novels are fiction, right?"

"But people don't want to read about fiction that's not feasible. So, there must be a place where you can hire wedding dates. Just tell her you want to hire a wedding date person that you don't want to take to a wedding, you just want to use as a decoy."

"Why don't you just come with me, and you can rebuff the efforts of my mother and step between me and whoever she is."

"She's probably really nice, and beautiful, and perfect for you."

"In which case, she'd have been married ten years ago, and even if she is, I'm not interested in her. She probably has warts on her nose or something."

"Warts on her nose wouldn't be nearly as bad as warts on her character."

"I don't care where the warts are, I'm not interested."

"She might not even have warts."

"You can stop arguing with me!"

Joanna would argue with a dead person. Seriously. She was that bad. Although, she claimed it was him. Was she right? Did he argue?

"Aren't you going to say anything?" he asked, feeling bad because he raised his voice enough that a couple of people had turned their heads to look at them. They looked back as soon as they'd seen it was just him and Joanna, used to their antics.

"You said to stop arguing. So I did."

"All right. Never mind. It just gets creepy when you get quiet."

"You are only calling me creepy because I called your mom creepy and you're trying to get me back."

"I agree with you that my mom is creepy, at times. Not all the time."

"Yeah. Not all the time. She was actually kind of nice to us once in a while."

"I can remember a couple of times she was nice. They were bookended by creepy or meanness, but still, I remember them."

"That's all you have to do. Remember them and give her credit for them."

"Are you going to answer my question?"

"I can't remember what your question is. I'll answer it as soon as you remind me what it was."

"Go with me. Run interference for me. Protect me. That's your job as my best friend."

"Fine. I'll go with you, run interference, and I'll protect you. But you owe me. Big time. Because your mom hates me, and I'm going into the mouth of the lion's den, because of my great loyalty and love for you."

"I don't believe that for one second. You agreed to go, and you must have ulterior motives. You always do."

"I haven't been to a rodeo in forever, and I want food. Good food. So you're going to cook for me the entire time I'm there."

"Done. Rodeo and food. You're so easy."

"I should have held out for something more. But not until spring. Can your mom wait until spring?"

"She can. I'll tell her, and we'll make plans to go. And I do appreciate it," he said, smiling down at her. She did argue a lot, and maybe she was a little bit cheerful like all the time, which could really get on a person's nerves, since there were times where a man just wanted to be quiet, like first thing in the morning when he first got up. He didn't want to be inundated with cheerfulness the way Joanna did.

Still, she was imperfect, and that made her perfect. Because he wasn't perfect either, and if he was looking for someone who was, they wouldn't want him.

"It looks like pretty much everyone's done eating. I think we can start cleaning up?"

"I can't wait until you have kids, because once you do, then you don't have to be the person who serves and the person who cleans up and the person who carries everything in from the car and all that other stuff."

"If you have kids, I'll help you with your kids, and someone else can do all the stuff that we do. Personally, I'm not sure I want kids."

"Why not? You're so good with them. Those kids yesterday, all five of them were eating out of your hand."

"You're the one that's good with kids. I just reap the benefits of them falling in love with you."

"No. I'm pretty sure it was all you."

"Regardless, kids are a lot of work, and before I have kids, I have to find someone to have them with, and I don't think I'm ever going to find anyone who compares to my brothers and you. I mean, who could measure up?"

"That's a pretty high standard," he said, which earned him a smack on the arm from Joanna.

"You're arrogant."

"You're violent."

"You insult me all the time."

"And you love me. A lot. If we get this stuff gathered up, we might have time to run into town and grab ice cream before we have to go back to the farm to do chores."

"You said the magic words."

He grinned. Joanna would do anything for ice cream.

Chapter Twenty-Three

Tosha closed the book and kissed the foreheads of her daughters. River barely stirred, and Bailey smiled sleepily. She wasn't sure whether they understood exactly what happened or not. That their mother had gotten married. Or maybe they'd had so many men in and out of their lives they just didn't care.

What had happened to her vow to stay away from men?

She was slowly pulling the door closed as Tobias came out of Mitchell's and Phoenix's room. Phoenix was already asleep. Mitchell had really taken to Tobias.

"They good?" he asked softly as the door clicked closed behind him.

She nodded.

"Would you want to go downstairs for a couple of minutes?" he asked, and she nodded again, although that question sent a swirl of nervousness through her. Neither one of them had talked about how marriage would change the relationship. They hadn't had time. They had gone to the hospital after the morning chores were done, visited with Gram, talked to the doctor some, and then told Gram what was going on. She didn't seem the slightest bit surprised, and it seemed natural since she was the one who had told Tosha what Tobias had planned to begin with.

The pastor had wanted to do marriage counseling, and after that, they got married. Tobias's family wasn't going to allow that to go by without having a meal and a celebration. That had taken longer than Tosha had expected, but she hadn't had to cook supper because they'd brought the leftovers home. They had enough for tomorrow too. She was going to have to figure things out and scrape together some money for groceries at the very least. It would be nice to get Phoenix a crib so he wasn't sleeping in a pack and play anymore too. And Gemmy and River could use a bed since they were sleeping on an air mattress on the floor. But none of that was essential.

She was just happy to have a roof over their heads.

"Coffee?" Tobias asked as she walked by him down the stairs.

"I might take a little bit of tea. Something to soothe my nerves a bit. It was quite a day."

"It was, although I'm not sure what it says about me that you marry me and now you need something to soothe your nerves."

"I guess I just...have a lot of bad memories associated with marriage. Although I've never had marriage counseling quite like that."

"Where the pastor talks about what the Bible says about men and women's roles in marriage?"

"And the idea that you're to be kind to your spouse before you're kind to anyone else. Kinder to your spouse than you are to anyone else."

She walked to the kitchen and put the teakettle on the stove. "Would you like some?"

"No, thanks. I might get a glass of water later, but I'm good for now."

"Your nerves are fine?"

"That was my first time getting married, so I was a little nervous, but I also felt a calmness, and I'm pretty sure that's because I know it's what God wanted me to do. I'm not sure why, but...it was clear He did."

"It still amazes me that you just do whatever He tells you to."

"I guess what's amazing to me is that He even bothers to tell me to do anything. Who am I? And yet, the God of the universe cares about me and guides my life. That's humbling."

"I don't know, He gave me to you, so He mustn't care about you too much."

"I think that shows just how much He does care about me. More than I thought He did."

"You're just saying that." She couldn't help it though, the comment warmed her heart. Did he really think that she was actually something special? He couldn't. He couldn't possibly look at her life and look at her and think that there was anything there worth admiring.

"I like how you decided to change. But you weren't so stiff-necked in your change that you couldn't see that maybe there was something else, something that you need to bend a little for."

"You're talking about my vow to not have anything to do with men or marriage again, and then, two days after I met you, I agreed to marry you."

"Yes, I am. I mean, I admire you for wanting to change, and then I admire you for being able to see that maybe you made a change too far in the wrong direction, and you adjusted. Sometimes, like my sister Joanna apparently told you, I decide something, and I refuse to change, even though I know I would be better off if I would just let go and do the reasonable thing."

"But sticking with something takes courage and responsibility. So there's that."

"True. But I suppose wisdom is knowing when to stick and when to let go."

"I suppose we could all use wisdom." She wouldn't mind having more.

"Wisdom is something you gain with age and experience. And suffering. Suffering often brings wisdom."

"So you're trying to tell me that something good comes from suffering?"

"Don't you think so?"

Her teakettle started to whistle, and she hadn't even gotten a tea bag out.

She did that while turning off the burner and then pouring some water into her cup so it steamed.

"How is this going to work?" There. She asked the question that was most on her mind.

"This? You mean you and me?"

She sat down in a chair, and he pulled a chair so he was catty-corner from her, so they could sit close and talk. It was almost too close. She was already a little nervous, and his presence so near made her stomach squeeze even harder.

"Yeah. I mean, we barely knew each other, now we're married. I was standing there in front of the preacher thinking I should have asked for a week or something, but we didn't have the time."

"You have as much time as you want. We don't have to...be married, not in every sense of the word, until you're ready."

"What if I'm never ready?"

He didn't seem fazed by her question, but he did look into her eyes. Studying them, or maybe he was just trying to figure out an answer.

"I guess I hadn't thought of that. What do you think? Are you ever going to be ready?"

"I suppose I won't have a choice. It would hardly be right to marry you and then want you to pretend that we're not married for the rest of your life."

"We're already living together."

"I was surprised when I realized that you were living with my gram. I didn't even know it."

"The past few days were so full of different things that one slipped by. But yeah. I moved in a few months ago. I can take you and show you my cabin. It's...not nearly big enough for a family of seven."

"That must be hard for you to wrap your head around."

"Remember I came from a family of fourteen, so this is only half of what I grew up with."

"I love that smile. Your whole face changes whenever you smile."

Her comment made him grunt. "I guess I'm not sure what to say about that."

"You can say thank you." Was he not used to receiving compliments? Maybe he wasn't used to receiving compliments from a woman. His one experience with a woman wasn't very good. Could she give him an experience that was different?

"Thank you."

She laughed because he said it simply, just what she told him to.

"I like it when you obey," she said, and he laughed, at her obvious play on what the pastor had told them.

"The pastor said that was your job, not mine."

"So we're doing some role reversal here. Is that a bad thing?"

"Do I have to answer the question? I mean, can't I plead the fifth or something?"

"I suppose if you feel the need to."

There was a little bit of laughter in the air, and she liked that. It was better than the tension and the seriousness and the nervousness that had gripped her soul. It loosened and made her feel like maybe, just maybe, being with this man would be better than being with anyone else in the world. That's what she wanted when she got married, to know that the person that she was married to was the person that she would rather be with, that if she had the choice of anyone in the world, she'd choose that person.

Marriage had never turned out that way.

"You know, I was trying to look at my marriages, and I'm embarrassed that I can say that in the plural, and think about the things I had done wrong, things that I wish I had done and that I feel contributed to their demise."

"I don't think that's a bad thing, but I don't know that you necessarily need to either. I'm not going to leave you, no matter how terrible you are. I'm just not."

"One of those things you made a decision on and nothing's going to change your mind?"

"That's right. My mom always called me stubborn, but I like to say I'm determined, or I have perseverance. I will be here forever. You're just not going to be able to get rid of me."

She laughed. Maybe she would have liked to have had soft words, pretty words, romantic words, telling her that he loved her and he couldn't live without her and he wanted to breathe her air and all of those other romantic things, but there was nothing better than someone who would never leave. After all, he wasn't claiming to be in love with her or even to like her, he was promising to stay no matter what. That was something that money could not buy.

Speaking of money... "When are we supposed to get paid?"

"I did some inquiring today. Apparently there's a website that you log into. There is a code in the letter, and I'm supposed to insert that code, and that will prompt them to do a search for our marriage certificate which the pastor was going to file at the courthouse today after we got married. I figured that I would give it a little bit of time to go through, and then I would register."

"And then after they see our marriage certificate, we...get the money?"

"Yeah. Apparently that's how it goes."

"Wow. I can't believe it would be that easy."

"I kinda suspect it won't be, because...when is anything ever easy?"

"Yeah. It always seems like you have to jump through a lot of hoops, despair of ever getting through it, and then finally figure out that hey, maybe it'll work out after all."

"Exactly. I'll just keep working until we get it. We're not going to let any hard hurdles stop us."

"Is that your philosophy in life?"

"I suppose. Just keep going. As long as you're sure that you're going in the direction that God wants you to go. That you're doing what He wants."

"You know, I've been thinking about that God thing."

"Okay?"

"I started talking to Him again."

"He wants to talk to you. He wants to have a relationship. With everyone. But especially you."

"Especially me?"

"He's calling you, isn't He?"

"I don't know about calling me, but He brought me into contact with you, which made me realize that I drifted away from Him. It was never Him who left me."

"That's a good realization. He's like a parent, I mean, all through the Bible, God is referred to as God the Father. You think about your relationship with your kids, and no matter how bad they are, what they do, you're never going to not love them. Not one of them. You'll always want to talk to them. You'll always want to have a relationship with your children. That's how God is with you."

"That's a really good example. Because you're right. Sometimes Mitchell gives me a hard time, but it doesn't matter what he does, I'll always love him."

"Right."

She took a sip of her tea and thought back over their conversation. The main thing that she had wanted to talk about, about how their marriage was going to change the relationship, hadn't exactly been settled. But he basically said that she could take as long as she wanted.

"What would be the sign that I've taken as long as I need and I am ready to...?"

He knew exactly what she meant, and she was grateful she didn't have to spell it out. From the way she was talking, a person would think that she didn't have five children.

"Why don't you just tell me? Would it be too hard?"

"You don't need time?"

"I suppose I do. But...I was thinking I would be courting you the whole time."

"Courting? But we're married. And what does courting mean anyway?"

"Maybe dating would be a better word. After all, we're married, so we can date, right?"

"Dating is something people do before they're married?"

"In my opinion, you should court before you're married, which is where you get to know someone, bring them to see your family, talk, but you don't spend a lot of time alone. Just know that both of you have similar goals and bonds and you are both aligned with the same ideas. Both going forward with the relationship that God wants for you. Dating is where you spend time alone, doing things by yourselves, which maybe isn't such a good idea for people who aren't married, because then the temptation to do things that you shouldn't do unless you're married is pretty strong."

"How do you get to be so wise?"

"I can't take credit for that. That's what my parents taught, and the older I get, the more sense it makes to me. I have to admit when I was younger, I didn't always think it was a good idea, but at least when things went down with Candace, my siblings all knew that I hadn't been spending any time alone with her unless I had snuck out of the house, because that was what we did. We did courting. So, it was a lot easier for them to believe that the baby was not mine and I had nothing to do with it. I was grateful for that teaching at the time. What if I had been alone with Candace? What if she had been seeing both of us? What if I could have been the baby's father? It would have been...a lot messier."

She sat at the table thinking. Obviously he'd gone over that in his mind, and his experience had solidified the wisdom of his parents at the time and he had taken it as his own.

"Do you think we can teach our children to court and not date?"

"I think so. We'll start now talking about it. I suppose that a lot of people who teach their children are disappointed when their kids choose something different. But up until they're eighteen, you can determine exactly what they're going to do. It's just the idea that once they're old enough to move out of the house and make their own decisions, it's nice if they internalize what you taught them, rather than thinking the world's way is better."

"My mom didn't want me to do the things I did, but like you said, I thought I had a better idea. I understand that mentality, and I'm not sure that there was anything that she could have done to fix it or to change it."

"I think that's the way things go a lot of times, and there's really nothing we can do about it. Kids have to make their own decisions. And all you can do is try to teach them as much as you can to do right, and hope that they love the Lord enough that they want to please Him, and they respect us enough to do what we want."

"So you don't think we browbeat them into submission?" she asked with a little smile.

"I don't know that a good spanking isn't in order at times. The Bible does talk about beating a child with the rod and saving his soul from hell. I'm not sure that some parents don't take that to the extreme when they shouldn't, but I also think that maybe we've gone to the extreme on the other end to where we raise children who do what they want because they're not afraid of any punishment."

"Sometimes punishment is the only thing that keeps us in line."

"Like what we were talking about before, where suffering begets wisdom. Punishment begets wisdom. I think that sometimes we as a society have done too much to keep our kids from suffering, and we ended up depriving them of gaining the wisdom that they should gain in their childhood, so they don't have to make those mistakes in adulthood."

"I've never heard it put like that before."

"Again, I can't take credit for it. A lot of it was my parents."

"I didn't listen to my mother the way you listened to your parents. I was arrogant and awful hard on her."

"I don't think it's wrong to tell our children that. Let them know that you made mistakes that could have been avoided."

It didn't escape her notice the way he said our children, like the children were both of theirs and he was taking responsibility for them.

"Do you really consider them 'our' children?"

He blinked, looking surprised. "Yeah. Of course. Why wouldn't I?"

"Because they're not really yours."

"But I want them to be. I'll be the dad. To all of them. I guess we didn't talk about custody and visitation."

"I picked such winners that is not really an issue. Mitchell and Bailey's dad might give us a hard time at times, but he's afraid to say anything because he's afraid that I'll make him pay child support. River and Gemmy's dad is in jail. Last I heard anyway, and I'm pretty sure he's going to get put away for at least ten years if he's convicted on his charges."

"Wow. You really did pick some winners."

"Then I had someone choose me. Someone who was a lot different than they were."

She wasn't sure what it was that she said, but it made him smile, like he was really pleased. She liked it when what she said made him happy. It was interesting, she didn't remember ever being happy to make any of the other men in her life happy. But making Tobias happy thrilled her to her very soul. That alone made him different.

Chapter Twenty-Four

Tobias stared at his phone as he waited for Tosha to text him back. She had gone in to see her gram who had been moved to the rehabilitation center today, exactly one week after her fall.

The money had come through, just as promised, and Tobias would have to have a conversation with Tosha about what they were going to do with it. Obviously, they couldn't spend it all, nor would he want to. But his family could use some, and they would be able to pay for her gram's care. Beyond that, he really didn't know what she might want to do. He didn't know anything about investing, and while he wouldn't mind buying land or cows or farm equipment with it, he hadn't even given that much thought. His main thought had been survival and helping the people around him.

All of the kids. Alaska has a baby of her own, Joanna and Phoebe will probably be around as well. It can be crazy over there.

He knew how his family was. The more nuts it got, the happier the women were. For some reason, having a bunch of kids running around having fun made them happy.

He enjoyed it too, as long as he could get away from the chaos. That wasn't entirely true; he loved his nieces and nephews and enjoyed spending time with them. But he preferred to do it in the summer when most of the crazy chaos was outside and didn't drive him quite so insane.

That's fine with me.

He texted Alaska back and let her know that it would be fine. She responded that Ezra would be over to pick them all up.

Now, the whole afternoon and evening stretched out before them with no children in the house. It was funny how the kids took up all of their time. He wondered if Ezra and Alaska had done this on purpose, knowing that he and Tosha had had very little time alone together since their marriage five days ago. Just in the evening after they put the kids to bed, and he could tell Tosha was always extremely worn out by that time. He hated keeping her up late.

For the first time in his life, he texted these words.

Would you like to go out?

He paused for a moment with his thumb hovering over the send button. Why was it so difficult to ask his wife, *his wife*, to go out with him? Maybe he was worried about what she would say. What would he do if she rejected him? That would make things awkward this evening. Goodness, it would make things awkward this afternoon when she came home.

But he couldn't live his life in fear of rejection. He would have to accept it if she said no and try to talk to her, figure out why.

With that thought, he hit send. Nothing ventured, nothing gained, wasn't that how the saying went?

It felt like it took her forever to respond as the children played around him.

Mitchell came out to the kitchen, just watching him, seeing what he was doing. He had been getting things out to make the chicken casserole for supper but decided against it once Alaska had invited the children over.

He smiled at the boy, who grinned back at him. Mitchell had been nothing but an angel since they moved, but Tobias wasn't fooled. The kid had a mischievous streak a mile wide. The thing was, he had a really great heart too. With the right guidance, the kid was going to grow up into a man of character and conviction who wasn't afraid to have fun.

He hoped he was up to the task. Being the father to such a talented and amazing child.

> That sounds like fun.

He felt relief as he lifted his phone. It washed over him in a great big cooling wave. He couldn't believe how he had sweated over her answer.

> I can do the evening chores early. Let me know what time you're going to be home.

Maybe he'd have time between the time Ezra came to pick up the kids and before Tosha got home.

He wasn't sure, he'd have to see.

She came back with a time that he thought would give him enough to at least get a good start on the chores.

> I'll see if I can get the chores done, then we won't have to worry about what time we get home.

He didn't know why it mattered. He didn't have any plans to do anything that would take them all night, but at least then they wouldn't have the pressure of needing to get back.

He realized as he stood there thinking about what he could do with Tosha that he probably should pack clothes for the kids if they were going to stay overnight. He was new at this kid thing, and he was glad that he had figured that out before Ezra was standing there expecting the kids to hop in the truck.

Phoenix started fussing waking up from his nap, so Tobias went in to get him and considered what he should send. Jammies and an outfit for the next day. Should he send anything extra?

He decided against it. Ezra and Alaska had kids around the same ages, and if any of his kids needed extra clothes, he was sure they would find something that would work.

They had gotten more than a foot of snow in the last week, and the kids would probably be out playing in it together. There were no hills to slide down, but there were plenty of other things to do in the snow.

He thought about the old snowmobile that he'd seen in Mrs. Wells's barn. Back when he was a kid in Wyoming, they'd had snowmobiles, and he thought that might be something that he and Tosha could do some evening after the kids had gone to bed.

There wasn't anything better than gliding over the snow with the moonlight shining down on the darkness all around. He always loved it, and suddenly he wanted to share that with Tosha.

He'd need to start working on it and see what he could come up with. Whether or not he could get it fixed and get it running. He wouldn't say anything to her until he was sure.

By the time Ezra arrived, Tobias had clothes for the kids packed in the bookbags that they'd bought them for school. Gemmy and River weren't going to school, but they'd gotten bookbags anyway. He filled Phoenix's baby bag with plenty of diapers, wipes, bottles, and formula and figured that Alaska knew what she was doing. He wasn't going to worry whether he sent enough stuff or not. Alaska would take care of them.

Ezra had married a good woman, a hard worker, and one that Tobias admired, despite her background. In fact, her background seemed like it was similar to Tosha's, although there were definite differences.

Regardless, he'd been shocked when Ezra had chosen Alaska, but Ezra had accepted his decision to marry Tosha with aplomb.

After the kids left, he put his outerwear on and went out to do the chores. Mitchell had been disappointed that he wasn't going to get to help that evening, and Tobias had to bite back a smile. At that age, helping was fun. Hopefully when he was actually old enough to be a help, he'd still want to.

He had done the same thing when he was a kid. He didn't remember his dad complaining about it or even saying anything, but he remembered clearly loving to help his dad, dogging his every footstep, and begging to be allowed to do things outside. So happy when his mom would let him out, to get away from the books and schoolwork and anything that had to do with being stuck indoors. Then, when he was a teen, knowing that it was his duty to help, it had lost its appeal, and he had taken every opportunity to take a nap.

It was funny how things changed.

He had just finished up and was walking on the path he shoveled between the house and the barn when Tosha pulled up to the house.

He increased his walking speed and was able to meet her as she walked up to the house.

"How's Gram?" he asked, looking at her familiar face, her rosy cheeks, the hair that flowed out from underneath the hat that she wore.

"She was in pretty good spirits. They've gotten the pain under control for the most part, and I think that really helps. She was much happier today than she was before." She smiled and looked over at him as they walked up the walk together. "I really appreciate you watching the children so I could go. It's...hard to get away from them sometimes."

"I enjoyed it. This is a slow time at the ranch, so they don't need me for too much, and I have a few things I can catch up on here for your gram, but nothing pressing."

"Are you saying you have time to go out with me?" she asked with a little smile on her face. He realized that him asking her to go out with him had made her happy. That was an...enlightening revelation. She actually wanted to spend time with him. Really? Could he be reading that wrong? Surely not. He was pretty sure he was right. That she enjoyed being with him.

The idea made his heart smile.

"I'm saying I'll make time to go out with you anytime. I was pretty happy when you said yes."

"You weren't kidding about dating me."

"I think dating should be something all married couples do."

"Nice. I'm not going to argue with that."

"I should have been proactive and asked Alaska and Ezra to watch the kids, but as soon as they said they were going to, I immediately thought about spending time with you."

"I like that. Thank you." They had reached the steps, stomping the snow off their boots before he opened the door for her to go in.

"Thank you," she murmured as she walked through the door with him following her. "Do I have time to take a shower?"

"You have as much time as you want to. You don't have to hurry or worry that the kids will interrupt you."

He noticed that she either took a shower early in the morning before the kids got up, in the evening after they went to bed, or she rushed through it sometime during the day when he was there to keep an eye on them.

Things did seem to be a little bit easier since they enrolled Mitchell and Bailey in school. But in a way, she had her helpers taken away from her. In another way, Mitchell wasn't constantly picking on everyone and creating chaos and dissension throughout the day.

With Mitchell, it was half good, half bad almost all the time.

"That sounds like such a luxury."

"If you'd rather spend the day taking a shower and don't want to go with me, I suppose that's okay. But I'll feed you if you go out with me."

"He's bribing me with food." She grinned. "It's working."

He smiled at her playful attitude and jerked his head. "I think I'll take a shower too. I'm finished with the chores, so I don't have to go back out once we get home, other than to check on everything."

"All right. I think we could race, but the luxury of being able to take a leisurely shower without having to worry about when the kids are going to need me is too alluring to resist."

"Take your time, if I starve to death, just kick my body out of the way, okay?"

"Are you trying to make me feel guilty?" she asked, laughing as she hurried upstairs.

He had been around Tosha enough to know that she might not rush the way she would if the kids were home, but she wasn't going to keep him waiting any longer than she needed to. She was extremely considerate that way. He tried to be the same.

He was unsure whether he succeeded or not. Maybe he should ask her. They should have plenty of time to talk tonight without being interrupted with children, and he had to admit, he was really looking forward to it.

Chapter Twenty-Five

Tosha didn't hurry exactly, but she didn't want to keep Tobias waiting. He was probably starving. It seemed like he was always starving. The nice thing about Tobias was that he would eat whatever she cooked. She wasn't the world's best cook. But if she set it on the table, he ate it.

She probably shouldn't compare him to all the men that she'd been with before, but she'd never had any of them who didn't care what she set in front of him and just ate it without comment and with thanks.

She didn't mind cooking for a man like that. In fact, that made it fun. She knew she could cook anything, and he would be okay with it. However, she was learning his preferences, and without him saying anything, she was trying to cook to those. Interesting that all the complaining in the world didn't make her eager to cook things that a man liked, but when a man showed appreciation the way Tobias did, she went out of her way to try to seek out what he enjoyed, just so she could cook it for him and see him smile.

She wanted to fuss over her hair and makeup and spend time on it. It was the first time in a long time she cared about how she looked and wanted Tobias to not be ashamed of her.

No, she didn't just want him not to be ashamed of her, she wanted him to look at her and see someone who was attractive and beautiful.

She swore she wasn't going to do that anymore. She wasn't going to let that dictate how she acted or what she wore or allow her to neglect her children in order to catch the eye of whatever man she was with.

But this was a little different, wasn't it? Since Tobias was her husband. After all, she wanted to please her husband. And there was nothing wrong with that. In fact, he went out of his way to please her, so shouldn't she return the favor?

Still, she couldn't figure out whether he would appreciate her looking good more than he would appreciate eating quickly. Finally she decided that she had fussed with her hair enough, and it was time for her to go downstairs so her poor husband could go somewhere and get something to eat.

He was sitting at the kitchen table when she walked in, and he looked up. She didn't think it was her imagination that he blinked and then smiled slowly.

"You look nice."

It was his expression more than his words that made her heart glow in her chest.

"Thank you. So do you." And that was true. He had on a button-down that looked newish, and as he stood, she noticed that his jeans looked the same. He already had his boots on, and he took his coffee cup to the sink, setting it carefully down with a clank.

"You didn't say where we were going. I hope I dressed okay." She wore a dressy sweater with a pair of jeans and the only nice pair of boots she owned. Her feet might be a little bit cold, because they were more fashionable than functional. In North Dakota, functional seemed to be the status quo, almost like it was in Sioux City.

She carried her coat, and as he looked around and said, "Are you ready?", she nodded and stuck an arm in the sleeve to put her coat on.

He moved around, and before she knew it, he had helped her, holding up the back of her coat so she could easily get her other arm in.

When was the last time someone helped her put her coat on? She couldn't even remember her mother doing that when she was little.

"Thank you," she said, and she knew she sounded breathless. It was because he literally took her breath away. It was a strange feeling, one that was a little heady and very nice.

"My pleasure."

There was a look in his eyes that said that that was the absolute truth. Her cheeks heated, and she was tempted to put her hands over them. Instead, she busied herself by pulling her gloves out of her pockets and focusing on putting them on her hands while he grabbed his coat and shoved his hands in it.

"Did you have any place specific you'd like to go?"

"It's such a treat to go out, I honestly don't care."

"I figured I would be feeding you. Do you have a favorite restaurant?"

"I don't even know what they have in Rockerton. I guess I should have been looking around while I was visiting Gram, but I just wasn't."

"All right then. I'll decide today. Although we could go to the diner in Sweet Water if you're in a big rush to get back. It's not as long of a drive."

"What do you want?" she asked, feeling like she was a teenager on her first date. Isn't that what they said? And they argued about who had to decide where they were going. She really would choose, if she had any idea.

"Good food. We can go to the diner with the kids sometime. It's not fancy, and they're very family-friendly."

"Good to know, although by the time we get all the kids in and fed, we'll be exhausted."

"That's a good point."

They grinned at each other, and she knew that he knew exactly what she was saying. None of the other guys that she'd ever been with had ever helped her the way he had.

She wanted to tell him that, but he was holding open the kitchen door, and she took a breath and then walked through. She didn't know why she was nervous. They were already married. She wasn't trying to impress him at all. In fact, he already knew the important things about her. And she knew that he would work hard, that he fed her gram's stock every day and took care of all of the outside issues. He fixed a window that had been broken and had unplugged the dryer vent as well.

She only had to ask once. Maybe that would wear off, where he would ignore her when she asked him to do things or to help her, but so far, he'd been very solicitous and sweet.

To her surprise, he walked to her side of his pickup and opened the door for her.

"Thank you. Wow."

"We can take the SUV if you want to. I had a nicer pickup, but I traded it in when I knew that I was going to be going to get you."

"This is fine," she said, shrugging her shoulder, but his words went round and round in her head. He had traded in his truck before he even asked her to marry him? It was true, he had. Because he'd shown up in the SUV to pick them up.

As soon as he got in and started the truck, she said, "Did you trade your pickup in for the SUV just so you could haul all my kids around?"

She thought maybe there was a flush underneath his tan. "It was a little presumptuous of me, wasn't it?" he said. "In hindsight, maybe I should have asked the lady before I started buying vehicles to accommodate her family."

She wasn't quite sure how she felt about that. On the one hand, he had obviously been sure that she was going to say yes. On the other hand, he hadn't held onto anything, because surely he would rather be driving his nicer pickup, whatever that was, than this older one or the SUV.

"I guess God told me to ask you, and I just assumed that you would say yes, since I was sure that it was because of the Lord." He lifted his shoulder as he started out the driveway. "I suppose I shouldn't have been so bold."

"I admire your boldness, your confidence, and your absolute surety that you are doing what God wanted. That's a little bit new to me, but it's very admirable."

Chapter Twenty-Six

Tobias put his fork down. He hadn't had such a great steak in a long time. Of course, he couldn't remember the last time he'd gone out to eat, and he had to say, the company was far better than the steak.

"So is it good?" he asked, pointing to the pasta dish that she had gotten. She'd only eaten about half of it before she put her fork down and declared she was giving up.

He had teased her that she needed to save room for dessert.

"It was delicious. I cannot eat another bite."

"That's too bad, because I was really looking at that chocolate cake and thinking I would get a piece. But I can't eat the whole thing."

He glanced at her over the table and gave her a lifted eyebrow.

She laughed out loud, and he loved the sound. She sounded so young and carefree, like she wasn't a mom of five children and worn down with weariness and care.

"You know what, I think I have enough room for a couple of bites of chocolate cake."

"That's the ticket," he said and gave the order to the waitress when she came by to ask if they wanted anything else.

"You're a chocolate lover?" he asked, knowing that most people liked chocolate, but he had a couple of siblings who couldn't stand it.

"I am. I definitely have an addiction. If there's chocolate in the house, I can't resist. I'll eat it every time. So it's best to just keep it far, far away from me."

"A little chocolate every day is good for the soul." He'd have to remember that she liked it.

"I don't disagree with that. It definitely makes me happier."

They stopped talking for a minute while the waitress brought the cake he'd ordered and set the bill down as well.

He ignored the bill for now and handed her one of the forks that were on the plate. "You first?"

"So I am the cupbearer?"

"Okay. If you insist I go first, I don't have a problem with that."

"Hold up. I'll go first."

He laughed as her fork slid smoothly down through the cake, and she put it into her mouth.

"I think I need another piece to really be sure I understand all the nuances and can tell you for sure whether it's good or not."

"That's a yes, it's awesome."

He took a bite as she laughed at him.

He couldn't remember the last time he'd had such a good time. Would it always be like this between them? Or was it just like this because they were getting to know each other? Was this the way every relationship was at the start?

He wanted to build something that lasted a lifetime. To have mutual respect and admiration for each other. To be courteous at all times, because familiarity could breed contempt, if they weren't careful. He wanted to be careful.

But every relationship started out with those good intentions. It was just a matter of doing this when he was five or ten or fifty years into the relationship, making sure that he continued to treat her as well as he could.

"You got quiet," she said softly, looking at him as if she were really curious as to what was going on with him.

He didn't mind having someone who seemed to want to know what was going on in his head. Although he had to admit that sometimes there was nothing going on in his head. It was just full of stuff that he couldn't put words to.

"I was wondering earlier if you and I should talk about how we're going to split the money. But that doesn't seem like something a person should talk about on a date."

"I don't think we ought to have taboo subjects while we're out. If it needs to be talked about, we can talk about it. Maybe when our children are older and we have a little bit more alone time, we can designate date time for fun topics."

He didn't think they needed to wait until the children were older. They just needed to wait until they were sharing a room. After all, if they were in the same bed together all night long, they would have plenty of time to talk without being interrupted.

But he kept those ideas to himself. He didn't want to ruin the date by making her think that he was pushing for something she wasn't ready for.

"I guess I was thinking we should hire someone to invest it for us. But I was also thinking that maybe we should ask Sawyer and Ford what they did with their money." He held a piece of cake on his fork as he said, "I mean, I know that we're going to pay for Gram's care, and I had told you I had a couple of things I wanted to do for my family that will take the financial burden off Ezra's shoulders."

"I'm fine with that."

"But there should be plenty left over, and I don't want just one of us to be making the decisions."

"I think your idea of asking Sawyer and Ford what we should do is a good one. If they have experience in this, that's more than what I've got. I've never had two nickels to rub together, let alone money in the bank that I didn't know what to do with."

"I've saved up at times, but then I ended up spending it when I saw someone who needed it more than I did."

She didn't say anything but watched as he put another piece of cake in his mouth. She looked at him like he had grown two heads.

"What?" he asked.

"I guess I just never met anyone who handled their money that way.

Where they gave to other people the money that they were going to spend on themselves. It's impressive."

"Don't let it impress you. There are lots of times where I wished that I would have kept it for myself. Like when I brought you and the children home. I would like to have a home to bring you to, but we're staying with your gram. I'm sure she doesn't mind right now while she's not home, but... I don't know how she'll feel about it when she does come home."

"She's the one who invited me to stay with her."

"I know. I guess... I wasn't in the equation at the time, although she did ask me to help you."

"Marrying me was above and beyond the call of duty," she said, although she didn't seem to be upset about it.

"It's what God wanted." And then, for some unknown reason, he added, "It's what I wanted too. I can't explain why, because I'm not sure, but when you said you didn't want to marry me, I was...not devastated but disappointed for sure. And I don't think it was just the rejection. I couldn't figure out why, because after all, I was just asking you because God wanted me to. Why did I care? But I did." He paused for a moment and then said, "Thank you. Thank you for saying yes. I always seem to have a good time when I'm with you."

His words made her glow. He could see the change in her, and he tucked that away in his mind, along with the chocolate that she liked and the snowmobile ride. His wife liked words. Sometimes he didn't have them, but he should find the ones that he needed to in order to make her glow like that. But they had to be sincere, true words. He couldn't just tell her something just for the sake of trying to make her happy, when it wasn't true.

As they sat with the empty plate between them, he cleared his throat and said, "Would you like to take a walk after we're done here?"

She smiled and nodded. And then, while he still had his nerve, he said, "Would you be interested in going out with me again?"

She chuckled softly, and he found humor in those words too, although he hadn't meant them like that to begin with. After all, he was her husband. Hopefully she would be interested in doing this with him again.

"I'd love to."

She didn't give him a hard time for asking his wife out on a date, like she might turn him down. He didn't know. But while they were talking about it, he said, "Does it have to be at night? Can we go out during the day?"

"I'll do anything. Whatever you want."

"What do you want?"

"It's just a treat to get away from the kids. I love them. Don't get me wrong. But I've enjoyed getting to know you. And you made me feel special with the way you treated me tonight. That was nice too." She seemed a little shy as she said that last part. And he had the feeling that she really did appreciate the fact that he had been kind to her. To him, it was just the way a person should treat other people and most especially their spouse, but he supposed that maybe that hadn't been the way she had been treated in her other relationships.

"All right then. I'll let you know when I line up another sitter. That's one nice thing about having so many siblings, I can get a different sitter every week, and they'll only have to do it once every three months or so."

She laughed and shook her head, and he appreciated the fact that they could share some laughter together and enjoy their time. That she seemed to enjoy being with him as much as he enjoyed being with her. He wasn't just asking her to do it again because she was his wife and he had to. He was finding that he was hard-pressed to think of anyone else he'd rather be with. And that was the truth.

Chapter Twenty-Seven

"Thanks so much for letting us come. It's such a nice break to be able to see the kids playing happily." Agathe walked into Tosha's kitchen along with Joanna, who had stopped at her house to pick her up and left Phoebe to sit with Jim, Agathe's husband who was suffering from Alzheimer's.

"It's my pleasure. I haven't had the luxury of having visitors and getting to cook for them, and I had a really good time this morning making soup and desserts and homemade bread, and I'm not sure how everything turned out." Tosha's eyes glowed, and she looked like a happily newly married woman, even if she did have five children. Although two of them were in school, so only three of them were at home. Two little girls and a little boy who already sat in a high chair, playing with cereal. Agathe had never been blessed with babies, so it was refreshing to see the little ones so rosy cheeked and happy.

Taking care of her husband had become extremely difficult since he no longer knew who she was most of the time. Those few and far between moments when he looked at her and seemed to know her were becoming more and more rare.

"It looks like married life is treating you pretty well," Joanna said to Tosha as they settled themselves at the kitchen table, and Agathe breathed a sigh of relief, blowing out the tension and worry that accumulated as she cared for her husband day in and day out.

"It's been wonderful," Tosha said, and it was obvious she was telling the truth as a little blush stained her cheeks. "Tobias is so sweet, and he is always looking for ways to help me. Even though he's working on the family farm, plus taking care of all of my gram's animals and watching the kids so I can go see her every day."

"I heard you guys went out on a date," Joanna said, and Agathe felt a little longing in her heart for the days when she and Jim used to go out.

"We did. We just went out to eat, but Phoebe is coming tonight to keep the kids and we're going somewhere. He hasn't told me where we're going. He said it was a surprise."

"That's romantic. I would never have thought of Tobias as a romantic person," Joanna said, and then she looked at Agathe. "I always thought Jim was romantic."

"Oh, he was. I was just thinking about how we used to take the motorcycle and go for long rides during the summer. And one winter, we rode the whole way down to Florida. It was...unforgettable."

"When I'm riding with Stonewall, sometimes he'll have in his head that he needs to get there as fast as we can, even though there's no rush. I kinda think that's a man thing because my brothers do that too. Like, they need to go in a straight line from point A to point B. That kinda defeats the point of a road trip."

Agathe nodded. "Jim was never like that. We always stopped at all of the out-of-the-way places. We found some really fun restaurants and saw some great scenic places that most people miss."

She closed her eyes and thought about the waterfalls they'd seen, the covered bridges, the cute little hole-in-the-wall restaurants where the owner sat at the counter and chatted with customers as they came in and out all day. Those were the days.

And yes, it was sad that they would never do those things again, but she had those beautiful memories. Jim had been a really great husband.

They sat and ate the delicious bread and soup and enjoyed some dessert, while they shared laughter and stories and the little girls ran around the table, smiling and happy and unaware of just how blessed they were to have such a warm and cheerful home.

Shortly after that, she and Joanna left so Joanna could drop her off at her Alzheimer's support group meeting.

Joanna would go back and help Phoebe keep an eye on Jim during the meeting time and be back to pick her up.

Waylon had offered to take her multiple times, but she kept turning him down. It just seemed wrong to do something with the man even though her husband didn't even know her anymore. But she couldn't deny that she felt drawn to Waylon. He understood what she was going through, having gone through it himself with his wife, losing her not long ago. He still went to the meeting sometimes and had been a great source of support. But... She supposed her feelings for him were developing into something that a married woman shouldn't feel for a man who wasn't her husband.

She had struggled about whether or not it was wrong. After all, the Jim that she knew wasn't really with her anymore. He was gone, and he was never coming back. But...in a way, he was still here. And sometimes she caught glimpses of him. And even though she was more his maid, his servant, than his wife anymore, and she longed for a gentle touch, a little affection, a fun word, a little laughter, even a trip to the grocery store where they did it together, someone to share the workload, it didn't matter how much she longed for all of those things, it was wrong to look for that type of affection and comfort in a man who wasn't her husband.

Although she was pretty sure Waylon would be willing to take her anywhere she wanted.

Whether or not he would be willing to do more, she wasn't sure and didn't want to know. At least that's what she told herself. There were times where she really did want to know. Where she was tempted almost beyond words to reach out and just see if he would hold her hand for a bit, sit with her, be a companion, and give her a break from the dark and dreary days of making sure her husband didn't leave the house and cleaning up after him, messes she couldn't have imagined as a young wife.

"There does come a time when we have to ask ourselves, when we're taking care of our loved ones at home, is it time to put them into a skilled nursing facility so they can get the very best care? It's exhausting for one person to do everything, and especially if you don't have any help, this should be something that you take into consideration."

Agathe gave her attention to the leader as she spoke. Typically, their meetings covered anything and everything, from taking care of their loved ones to feeling lonely and unloved, left behind, or even resentful of the fact that they were the ones doing all the work and who was going to be left to take care of them?

But she had been considering putting Jim in a facility for a while now. Twice, he had gotten out of the house in the middle of the night, but thankfully it hadn't been cold enough for him to suffer any harm. And she had found him easily in the morning. The neighbors had seen more of her husband than they ever cared to, but at least he was safe.

He had gotten "lost" several other times, where she'd been panic-stricken until friends and neighbors had helped her find him.

Since then, she'd changed the locks on all the doors to the type of knob a person had to put a code into in order to get the door open. It was a pain, but Jim couldn't remember the code, even though she'd told him multiple times, because he would get upset and angry with her if she didn't.

And that was probably the worst thing. Jim's anger. Back before Alzheimer's, he was kind and patient and sweet. Romantic like Joanna had said today. Just the best husband ever. But the disease hadn't just taken his memories and his awareness, it had taken his personality and changed it into a man who was short-tempered and grumpy.

She supposed she should just be thankful that it wasn't the way he normally was, and she had a beautiful marriage with a wonderful man, and now she was getting to experience something of what other women must have experienced. Women who put up with men who were short-tempered and nasty. She didn't really feel like she'd signed up for that. She hadn't married a nasty, short-tempered man. She'd married her Jim, sweet and beloved, kind and always ready with a smile and a helping hand.

Now, she felt lonely and alone.

"That was a pretty good meeting. I struggled with that with my wife. Whether to put her in a facility or not. It felt like I wasn't doing right by her if I did." Waylon came up to her and put an arm around her, maybe just to steady her as he helped her navigate through the chairs to the door.

She slid away from him, reluctantly, because she wanted to stand and savor the feel of the strong arm holding her, someone actually being courteous and helping her.

"I wonder about that myself. I suppose it's been timely, because three times in the last week, Jim's been up in the middle of the night, and if it weren't for the locks on the door, he would probably have been outside and frozen to death." She gave Waylon a smile, hopefully easing the sting of any rejection he felt when his hand slipped away from her shoulders and fell to his side as she moved away from him. "Thank you for helping me put those locks on the doors. They've been invaluable."

"This time of year, you don't want him to be outside. North Dakota nights can be brutal from now until March or April."

"Some years, it's even longer," she said, knowing that she loved the land that her husband had moved her to, but she also missed the beautiful French countryside of her childhood. Waylon had offered to take her to visit it, and it was so tempting for her to take him up on it. She might not be able to travel by the time Jim passed away. But she couldn't travel with a man she wasn't married to. Not when her husband was still alive. That just wasn't right.

"If you need a ride home, I can give you one," Waylon said solicitously as they moved out of the community building, toward the outside door and the parking lot.

"Joanna Clybourn is waiting for me. I am riding home with her. She's expecting me."

She stumbled over her words a bit, uncomfortable and also fighting hard against the urge to take him up on the offer. They'd gone out for ice cream once or twice, but she felt so guilty about it that she hadn't gone again. She just couldn't do that to Jim. It wasn't right.

"I get it. But as he fades, you're still here in the land of the living. It's easy to get discouraged and depressed, and I just want you to know that there are people around who care about you and who will support you and do fun things with you. The world doesn't have to be a completely gloomy and sad place."

She nodded her head but didn't speak. He painted a good picture, and she was more tempted than she wanted to admit to take him up on it. Opening the door for her, he waited for her to walk through and then followed her out. Thankfully Joanna waited right by the end of the sidewalk, and she didn't have to stand and wait for her or fend off any more of Waylon's offers.

"It was nice to see you. Maybe I'll see you at the next meeting."

"Maybe. I've been thinking about heading to Florida for the winter. I could use a little sunshine, and a buddy of mine who lost his wife over the past year has offered to let me come down and share his RV."

"That sounds really fun. I'm happy for you."

"I worry about you, you know. I haven't given him an answer because... I didn't want to leave you up here alone."

She wasn't sure whether he was on the verge of offering for her to go down. Surely he knew she wouldn't.

"If you put Jim in a facility, you would have more freedom." He smiled, a caring, kind smile. The kind of smile that Jim used to give her. It made her feel like...he truly was concerned about her. But surely he knew that there was no way she was going to put her husband in a facility and go to Florida for months at a time?

"I'm thinking about it. Mostly because the work is hard for me, and I know I'm not doing as good a job as what someone else would do. The whole reason that I kept him home to begin with was because I knew I could take care of him better than anyone else. But at this time... I'm not sure."

"There comes a point where that has to be a consideration. I'll see you at the next meeting, then I'm not so sure I'll be around after that."

She nodded and then turned to Joanna's car. Joanna had gotten out to open the door for her. The kind move, the sweet consideration almost brought tears to her eyes. How she longed for a gentle touch. How she longed for someone to care about her and for her to not have to be the strong one all the time.

For now, this would have to be enough. This and her faith that God cared. Even if He couldn't give her a hug or a pat on the back or sit on the porch swing with her, He was enough. And that had to be okay.

Chapter Twenty-Eight

"So what is this place?" Tosha asked as they pulled into the cabin that Tobias had made for himself by hand.

He had gotten his siblings to come earlier than normal to watch the kids so that Tosha could see it in the daylight.

He watched her face carefully. He was pretty sure she liked it.

"It's the cabin I built. It's where I lived before I moved in with your gram."

"You built this?" she asked, her eyes getting wide, and he enjoyed the shocked expression on her face.

"I had a little bit of help with the trusses. My brothers came occasionally and gave me a hand. But otherwise, I did pretty much everything myself."

"Well. You are a spectacular carpenter." She looked again at the home, and he smiled hugely on the inside, although he only allowed a little smile to tilt up his lips.

"You haven't seen anything yet. I finished the inside myself too."

"Oh my goodness. I'd love to see it!" she said as they stepped away from the vehicle and walked up the walk. He had paved it using natural stone, and while it was slightly uneven, it was also rustic and beautiful. At least to him. He had hoped that Tosha would enjoy it as well.

"Is this on the Sweet View Ranch property?" she asked, naming the ranch that his siblings shared together.

"It adjoins it. It's about forty acres that didn't go with the ranch that I bought myself."

"So you always planned to live off of the ranch?"

"I love my siblings, but I guess I like having a place where I can go where it's quiet and away from the chaos."

"You're an introvert. You can be around people, but you get energized when you're alone."

"That explains it," he said. He'd heard the word before, and knew it applied to him, but didn't really think about it too much. He just needed to be alone sometimes. And he knew that about himself. Although, with five children, he was going to have to learn to accept the fact that there would be chaos more often than not. Because no matter where he moved, the kids were coming with him.

Until they left.

Unless they had more children. They hadn't even talked about that. That might be an uncomfortable topic, although the last date that they'd been on, where they'd gone to the diner in Sweet Water and then walked under the stars on the ranch, had been amazing. It seemed like he and Tosha always had something to say, or the silence was comfortable and not awkward at all.

He felt comfortable enough that he figured he could probably talk to her about that.

As they reached the steps, he reached down and slipped his fingers into hers. He hadn't really even thought about it, but as he did it, he glanced at her to see what her reaction would be.

To his surprise, she looked at him and smiled.

"I like that," she said, and it sounded sincere.

"I've been wanting to do it for a while, but I was kind of waiting until you said something. I...wasn't even thinking about it just now. It felt natural."

"It feels natural to me too, and I'm sorry that you are waiting on me. I guess I'm learning to follow your lead, and it feels weird to take the lead in something when I'm trying to train myself to submit to your authority the way the pastor said."

The pastor had talked about that, and he had specifically looked at Tosha and told her that she needed to be careful of the man that she married, since she was commanded by the Lord to submit to his authority. It wasn't something that the pastor chose to tell her, it was something that was in the Bible, written in black and white. A person either had to decide that they were smarter than God, and they could pick and choose what they believed from the Bible, or they needed to obey what the Bible said.

Tobias wasn't sure what Tosha was going to decide, but apparently, her shift toward the Lord had included the idea that she needed to listen when God gave a command.

Tobias only hoped that he was the kind of man who deserved her submission. Because the pastor had also said that he had the harder job of the two of them, since he was to love his wife as Christ loved the church and gave himself for it. He could spend the rest of his life trying to do that.

He opened the door and allowed her to walk in ahead of him, and somehow they held hands the entire time. He hadn't held hands with anyone before, and he found himself loving the feel of her hand in his, the idea that she was right beside him, close. When they had the kids, it was harder because their hands and arms were full of wiggly children and helping in one way or another, or carrying all the things that the kids needed them to carry.

But now, on one of their dates, he was free to touch her as he wanted.

She was okay with him holding her hands, she might be okay with him...putting his arm around her, even kissing her.

The idea gave him a strange thrill that shot the whole way to his toes.

He definitely needed to stop thinking about that, or he wasn't going to be interested in showing her anything, but rather, he'd spend his time trying to figure out how he could get her to kiss him.

"You did all of this?" She glanced around the room, at the tongue-and-groove walls, the butcher-block countertops that he made himself, and the cupboards that he also crafted by hand.

He'd laid the tile on the kitchen floor and done the tile in the showers as well.

"Do you enjoy the work?"

"I do. That's how I ended up at your grandma's house. She had some things that needed to be fixed, and I just started giving her a hand with them. And it led to more, until we developed a friendship, and from there, I started helping her with her farm things too."

"Gram was really blessed to have you. Every time I visit her, she asks about you and how you're doing. She also asks about our marriage. She wants to make sure you're happy. Sometimes I'm not sure she even remembers that I'm the one that's actually her granddaughter."

"She loves you. I can tell you for sure that she does."

"I know. I'm just teasing. Because she really does think the world of you, too."

She looked down and bit her lip, and he thought that maybe she had something more to say. When he waited and she didn't say anything, he prompted her.

"You have that look on your face that says you're thinking about something and you can't figure out how to talk about it."

"That's a look? And you recognize it?"

She seemed to love it when he read her looks and noticed things without her having to say anything. It actually did take a little bit of effort on his part, and sometimes he didn't put that effort in, but it was worth it because it made her smile.

"I was just talking to Agathe earlier today, and she talked about how Jim had always fixed things around the house, and how now that he was getting worse, he couldn't do it anymore and her porch needed repairs. She asked if Joanna had any suggestions on who might be able to do it."

"I see. So you see someone who could use some help and—"

"I don't want to offer you if that's not something you enjoy, but I know that you're always willing to lend a hand."

"I do like to help. And to me, that's a good way for us to spend our money. Buying supplies and helping someone. If I don't miss my guess, she doesn't have a whole lot of money."

"No. When she asked Joanna if she knew anyone, she said that she didn't have a whole lot of money, and she wouldn't be able to afford a whole new deck. Just wanted the old one repaired so it wasn't so wobbly."

"It's pretty late in the season, but I can shore it up now, and in the spring, we can build her a whole new deck. I think it might be good for Mitchell to give me a hand if he's interested."

"I thought we could do that on one of our dates?" She looked at him uncertainly.

That made him smile. "You'd like that?" he asked, feeling a little bit of a thrill that his wife not only cared about their neighbors but was willing to use some of their precious time together to do something for someone else. He would be willing to take her out to eat every week or spend money on her, but she was asking for someone else.

"Yes. I think it would make her happy."

"Then we'll have to do that, and maybe we can slip in a meal at the diner as well."

That really made her smile. He knew she loved being able to eat without having to cook or clean it up. It seemed like such a luxury to her, and he loved that she appreciated such a little thing.

"That would be perfect," she said softly.

They smiled at each other, and he couldn't help the fact that his eyes shifted down toward her lips.

Before he got distracted, he tore his gaze away and looked around the house.

"There's only one bedroom. I made it large and nice, with a huge bathroom, but...this isn't big enough for a family of seven."

"I kind of thought from the outside when I saw it that it wouldn't be," she said.

"So I was thinking I would add on to it. But only if this is okay. It's not far from your grandma's house, especially if you walk through the field. It's only about a ten-minute walk."

"We're that close?"

"Sure. When you drive out the driveway onto the road and then drive down the driveway to your grandma's house, it feels further. But it's really not."

"That's good to know."

"It would take me a while to finish an add-on." He paused and then decided he would just plunge in. "I wasn't sure whether you were hoping that we would have more children or not."

It didn't feel quite as awkward as what he was afraid that it would. Although he did notice that her cheeks started to get red.

"What do you want?" she asked.

"I want what you want. This feels like a decision we should make together, and you should have a huge say in it, because you're the one who has to carry the children and take care of them once they're born."

She pulled a lip in and looked around the house again, although he doubted that she was seeing it. She seemed to be trying to gather her words.

Chapter Twenty-Nine

Tobias wanted to know if she wanted to have children. Tosha had thought about this off and on since they got married. She wasn't quite sure exactly what their marriage was going to entail, but she assumed that a discussion about kids would be something that they would have eventually.

"It's not that we can't afford them." She smiled, thinking that if they used a little humor in the situation, it might be easier.

As she figured, he grunted a laugh. "That's the truth."

She couldn't believe that the billion dollars had come, just like that, with no problems. She had honestly thought that it was a scam. But she knew that Tobias would stay married to her whether they got the money or not, so it honestly didn't matter a whole lot to her one way or the other. She hadn't said that to Tobias though, because he might care. After all, he was only asking her to marry him because of the billion dollars.

Although, he had been so sweet and kind to her, she almost felt like...he really liked her.

But that didn't have anything to do with children. She knew if they decided to have more, he would be there to help her.

She ran her thumb over the knuckles of his hand as it held hers while she answered, not meeting his eyes. "Sometimes as we are eating around the table together, I look at you and think how much I'd love to have a little boy with your smile, your work ethic, or how I would love to see you hold your daughter in your arms."

"I have three daughters I get to hold."

"How much I'd love to hold a daughter of yours." She knew he knew what she was saying, and that time, he didn't try to correct her. "Five kids is a lot, and I don't want to have more if children aren't something you love and enjoy."

"I loved coming from a family of twelve siblings. It was a pain in the butt at times, and there were fights and bickering, and sometimes we still don't get along. We definitely don't agree on everything. But my family is my foundation. It's where I go when I need a babysitter, who I ask when I need help. It's the place I go when I need to feel needed, and yeah, sometimes it's a pain because right now, I'm working on the family farm, and I'm also doing Mrs. Wells's work, and I want to start working on carving out a spot for my own family. Whether it's here, or whether we decide to do something else. I suppose we could stay with your gram."

"I think she'd like that. But I also think she'd be totally okay if we lived just over the hill too. And she might not realize how chaotic the house truly is. Once she moves back from the rehabilitation center, she might kick us out in short order."

He laughed, knowing that she was joking. Her grandma wasn't going to kick them out.

"But..." she said as his laughter died out. "About children." She spoke slowly. "I appreciate the fact that we're talking about it. I... I guess I'm content leaving it up to you or up to God, whatever. We have enough money to raise them, and you've been an amazing dad. I know you're going to be there with any children that we have. You'll be helping, and it won't be me by myself. So... I'm fine with anything."

"Do you *want* more?" he asked, emphasizing "want."

"I guess I do." She was kind of surprised. When she had sworn off having anything to do with men, she knew that would mean no more children, and she already had five, which was way more than normal Americans had.

"I just know that sometimes kids can keep a woman from being able to do certain things. Like have a career or just being able to go to the grocery store without making a big production out of everything. I don't want you to resent them or to resent me, thinking I'm forcing you to do this. Because I'm not."

"I feel like if we need to, we can hire someone. Although, I would rather take care of the children and let someone else do the cooking and cleaning, except I've really been loving the cooking, just getting to be able to buy groceries without thinking about how much money is in my account and whether or not it will stretch that far, and I can make whatever recipe I want, and it's just...luxurious."

He smiled at her choice of words, and she knew he looked pleased. It was his billion dollars, the letter had come to him, and he had provided for her. He had never acted like the money was just his, and there was more money in their checking account than she would ever be able to spend on groceries in one hundred years.

"Money changes things, doesn't it?" he asked, although his voice didn't sound happy about it. It just sounded...matter-of-fact. But there was still a twinkle in his eye.

"It does. I guess I just hope it doesn't change me for the worse, you know?"

"That's why I was so pleased when you suggested that we do something to help Miss Agathe. That is, in my opinion, using your money wisely. Laying up treasure in heaven, rather than here on earth."

They talked about it some and had decided that they weren't going to change their lifestyle, and they figured out a budget. Neither one of them thought that they could ever go through a billion dollars in a lifetime, but they also didn't want to try, and they wanted to have plenty of money left over to allow their children to go to college if they wanted to or to get a start in life some other way, if that's what they wanted.

Tosha had been fine with that. Just the idea that they had money in the bank was a new concept to her, and she still hadn't gotten used to it.

"I want to do Agathe's porch, but I was hoping next week our date could be going Christmas shopping. How do you feel about that?" he asked.

The sun had slowly been sinking down, and the room was filled in shadows and milky darkness, and as a gust of wind blew outside, she shivered.

"I'm sorry. There's no heat in the house. I have the water shut off." He moved, shifting beside her as his hand slipped out of hers, and his arms came around her.

She snuggled against him, wrapping her arms around his waist. He felt hard and strong and solid, and she leaned her head against his chest, wondering if life could get any better. She really didn't think it could.

"We just need music, and we can dance."

"I might step on your toes. I'd feel bad about that," he murmured, one of his hands going up and down her back slowly, lightly, a touch that showed affection and love more than anything else. Those kinds of touches had been few and far between for her. The men she had been with hadn't been overly interested in showing any kind of affection or gentleness to her. She could clearly see now the difference between them and the man in her arms right now, but at the time, she had been looking for men who were loud and brash and attracted to men who had flirted and said all kinds of things, made promises that she now knew they never intended to keep.

So different than Tobias and so much worse.

She silently gave thanks to the Lord for the man that He'd given her, because there was no other way for her to say it. It certainly wasn't anything she had done that had gotten her someone like Tobias.

They stayed like that for what felt like a really long time before Tobias broke the silence.

"I'd asked you once for kissing lessons. Have you given it any thought?"

She smiled against his chest. She'd been thinking about kissing him. Hoping that he wanted to, but afraid to ask. Maybe he didn't want to kiss her anymore. They'd been talking about children, and she knew how a person got those, so he must have been thinking something along those lines, but kissing really wasn't necessary.

"I definitely am interested in kissing lessons. Am I giving them to you, or are you giving them to me?"

He grunted. "I don't think the person who's never kissed anyone is supposed to be giving lessons on how to do it."

"I think that would be a nice way to upset the apple cart. Why don't you go ahead and give me a kissing lesson. I'll be your pupil, and then I'll tell you how you did afterward."

"As a teacher or as a kisser?" He grinned a little as he looked down at her. "Because you're making me nervous."

"There's no need to be nervous. I promise you, the bar is not that high." She rolled her eyes, but he might not have been able to see it as dusk continued to deepen into darkness.

"That doesn't make me feel any better, because you deserve the best. No matter where your bar is."

"I already have the best. He's holding me right now." She meant that with all of her heart. Maybe he heard the sincerity in her voice, because his head turned, and his lips settled on her temple.

"When I told your grandma that I knew a solution to your problem and then proceeded to let her know that I could marry you, I wasn't really thinking about you as a person, but I was thinking more about helping someone. In the only way I could. I mean, there were five kids who didn't have a dad and a woman who needed a husband. But ever since I met you, finally, three weeks ago, I've been impressed with you every time. I enjoy talking to you, being with you, and I find myself thinking about you when we're not together. When I go somewhere without you, I wish you were there. When I walk into the house, the first thing I do is look around to find you. I find myself pulling my phone out of my pocket to text you just stupid things you probably don't care about."

"I always love hearing from you."

"You might regret saying that," he said with humor in his voice. "I guess what I'm saying is I wasn't really expecting to feel loved. I was expecting to show it, to act it out, to live it in whatever way necessary, but I wasn't expecting these...feelings that I have. I... I... I'm falling in love with you." He hurried to add, "You don't have to say anything. You don't have to love me back. I am shocked, I guess."

"Why?"

"Maybe because we haven't known each other that long. Maybe because I would never have chosen you. Out of all the girls in the world, God chose you. I just did what God wanted, and...this fast beating of my heart, this anticipation that I feel any time I get to be with you, the way I just want to pull you tighter and never let you go, the way I can't stop thinking about you, I... I'm definitely infatuated. And if this is what being in love looks like, then I am. But whether the feelings go or whatever, I love you. I always will. I just want you to know that."

She was quiet for a few moments. She thought he was going to kiss her, and maybe he still was, but she appreciated the fact that he wanted her to know how he felt before he did. That he wasn't trying to push anything physical on her until she knew exactly where he stood.

"I think I fell in love with you the first time I saw you. I think it was the shaggy beard on your face that gave you a little bit of the desperado look, which clashed with the upright preacher boy look you have without even realizing it."

"Upright preacher boy?" he said, feigning hurt. "That doesn't sound like a compliment."

"That's exactly the kind of man I wanted, but that little bit of desperado just gives you a look that says dangerous teddy bear or something. I'm not even sure, but yeah. I had to remind myself over and over of my vow not to get involved with men from the moment we met. I suppose that says exactly where my feelings were going."

"I see."

"I love you. I want to make sure you know that. And I have no intention of changing my mind, no matter what your kiss is like." Maybe she shouldn't have said that last bit, but she wanted to remind him that she was expecting something.

"I think that was a hint."

"It was. I'm waiting."

"So this is my first lesson."

"No. It's my first lesson. You are the teacher." She lifted her head up, and there was just enough light for her to see his eyes sparkling down at her.

"Okay. The first thing you need to do is put your arms around my neck."

He didn't have trouble bossing her around. He was naturally a commanding kind of guy, even if he was quiet. She obeyed without a word. "Now, lift your face and pucker up."

"Pucker up?" she couldn't help but repeat, trying to hold back a snort.

"Whose lesson is this?"

"Yes, sir, kissing teacher."

"That's more like it." Maybe he was still smiling a bit as he lowered his head and gently touched his lips to her puckered ones. She couldn't help it, her lips broke into a smile, and she thought maybe he would give her a hard time for not obeying, but he seemed distracted by the feel of her lips on his, and before she knew it, they had settled more deeply, and she wasn't thinking at all about puckering or lessons or anything else beyond feeling his lips on hers and his shoulders under her hands and his body next to hers.

He lifted his head, running his lips over her cheek and resting them against her forehead. "Is it terrible that it makes me happy that our first kiss was here in this house?"

"Not at all. I think this house is going to be a place of many memories for us, and it seems appropriate for our first kiss to be here too."

"That's my hope. That it will be a house of many memories." He lowered his head and kissed her again, and it was a long time until either one of them felt the cold.

Chapter Thirty

"You can start putting the kids to bed at 7:30. By the time they get their teeth brushed and their jammies on and you read a few books, it'll be 8 o'clock and time for lights out." Mina watched as Tosha bustled around her kitchen. She was sixteen, and her Uncle Tobias and Aunt Tosha had asked her to watch the children for the evening so that they could go fix Miss Agathe's porch. Christmas was just a couple of days away, and the house had been decorated with gifts sitting underneath the tree. Tosha had already told her that she was going to have to watch Gemmy, the two-year-old, and River, the three-year-old, to make sure they didn't try to open the presents that were there.

After a few more last-minute instructions, Uncle Tobias and Aunt Tosha left.

Mina enjoyed playing with the children, and she enjoyed putting them to bed as well, holding the snuggly little baby, Phoenix, as he drank his evening bottle, and then reveling in the chaos as she diapered him and changed Gemmy and got the other kids in their jammies and read books to them all.

It helped take her mind off the fact that she wasn't going to school for another ten days. Which felt like a lifetime. Mostly because she wasn't going to be seeing Nash for all of that time.

He had rescued her from bullies and pretended to be her boyfriend. They were still pretending at school, but they never saw each other outside of school.

That helped keep it real for Mina, because she was finding it harder and harder to remember that the relationship at school was fake, only instigated by Nash for her protection. And that he didn't really like her as much as he seemed to as he held her hand and walked her around the halls.

She knew what adults all said about teenage crushes and first boyfriends and all that, and she supposed some of it applied to her because she really did have a huge crush on Nash. At school, she was allowed to act on her feelings, but outside of school, he didn't even text her.

"Good night, guys," she said softly as she pulled the door shut on the girls' room. She already said good night to the boys.

Now, as long as the children didn't wake up, she could do whatever she wanted to. Well, technically she could do whatever she wanted to. In reality, she had brought schoolbooks along, to get to work on the term paper her English teacher had assigned over the Christmas break.

Who assigned term papers over the Christmas break? Just the worst teacher in the world, that's all.

Actually, she knew that Mrs. Loveless really did care about her students and assigned the paper to her top English class because she knew that many of them were trying to get into good colleges and needed to work on their writing skills.

Mostly Mina didn't mind, but if she could get it over with here, where she wasn't missing out on any family celebrations, that would be just as well.

She had sat down at the kitchen table with her books open when her phone buzzed with a text.

Probably her mom checking on her.

But to her shock, the text was from Nash.

Meet me outside.

It wasn't a request; it was a command. She smiled and rolled her eyes at the same time. Then she texted back.

> I'm not at home.

I know.

> I'm at Uncle Tobias's and Aunt Tosha's house.

I know.

> You're outside here, now?

She lifted her head up and looked around. Was he really here?

Yeah. Come out.

She swallowed. No one had said she couldn't have any boys here. But she kinda figured it was an unspoken rule of her parents since she wasn't allowed to date at all. They had talked about courting, but everyone laughed at her at school when she even mentioned it, so she hadn't said a word since she was fourteen and hadn't even talked about it with her friends. She knew if she wanted to go out, she was going to have to sneak out. But she didn't want to do that to her parents. She respected them too much. Maybe she should have a talk with them and see if they would come around to her way of thinking. Because not doing what all of her friends were doing made her look like an idiot and a freak.

Still, she pushed all that aside. No one had told her she couldn't go out and meet with a guy if he came to see her, and there was nothing wrong with talking to him. It wasn't like she was bringing him in and making out on the couch.

Plus, the kids were already in bed, and the only thing she was missing out on right now was her schoolwork.

> I'll be right there. I need to put my coat on.

It was the fastest she'd ever put her coat and boots on, and it was barely a moment later that she was stepping outside into the magical full moon shining on the white snow making it seem almost like daylight. A romantic glow if she'd ever seen one. Made all the more so because there was an actual boy, the exact boy that she had a huge crush on, who held her hand between every class at school, outside waiting for her now.

"Nash?" she whispered as she stepped off the porch and onto the shoveled path. There were little boot tracks through all the snow, where the kids had played in the front yard. And there were adult tracks beside it, where Tosha and Tobias had walked around, playing with their children.

"Back here," Nash said, his voice coming from beside the house.

"What are you doing here?" she asked as she stepped off the path and into the snow, walking carefully over to the side of the house and getting the full effect of the moon as she came around the edge into the bright moonlight. The pole building that housed the hay hung low in the distance, and a few black figures out along the horizon showed where the cattle were.

"I wanted to talk to you. Is that so terrible? You don't sound happy to see me."

"I'm just surprised. I...missed you." It had only been a weekend and one day that they had been off.

He grinned at her admission. "I miss you too. I guess that's why I'm here. That, and this." He brought out a little box. It was wrapped with a pretty bow, and he held it in the palm of his gloved hand.

"That's for me?" she asked, a little bit of panic in her throat, because she hadn't gotten anything for him.

"For my fake girlfriend. I figured that people might ask you what I got you for Christmas, and you needed to have something to show them."

"I never thought of that. I don't have anything for you," she said, anxiety lacing her tone. She had a small amount of money saved up from birthdays and whatnot, and she had earned some money babysitting for her nieces and nephews, but usually she did that for free. It was just a family thing. She wouldn't dream of charging her aunts and uncles for watching their children. It was a privilege.

"You don't need money to buy what I want." His eyes were dark and glowing in the moonlight.

She blinked at him. What in the world was he talking about—

Her eyes opened wide.

When he saw that expression, he grinned. "Kisses are free."

Her mouth opened, and she didn't think to close it. She hadn't considered kissing him. Well, that wasn't entirely true. She definitely dreamed about that, but she hadn't considered doing it in real life. She kinda thought she would wait to kiss anyone until she knew she was going to be marrying him. Maybe even until their wedding day. But could she tell Nash no?

She swallowed and looked down at the snow. She didn't want to tell him no. Not really. But there was a huge part of her that did. Yeah, her parents had told her she couldn't date, and she had been thinking about trying to talk to them, but there was a part of her that really liked the idea of not kissing anyone until she kissed her husband. Could she really live a life like that?

She knew she would much rather go through life not having some random men walking down the sidewalk that she'd kissed, whose tongue had been in her mouth. What would she think when she was twenty or thirty or forty, and there were all kinds of men walking around who had been in her arms and whom she had kissed? Who were now married to someone else. How would she feel about that?

While she didn't think she would ever love anyone the way she loved Nash, her parents were right about infatuation being fleeting. Although, surely they didn't know the intensity of her feelings.

"What's the matter? Don't you want to kiss me?"

She looked up, unable to see the deep blue of Nash's eyes but easily seeing the strong shape of his jaw, the width of his broad shoulders, and the way he towered over her. He'd always been protective and kind to her. He'd never been anything but sweet. She didn't want to not give him what he wanted.

"I do want to kiss you. But... I made a vow to myself a while ago that I wasn't going to kiss anyone until I kissed my husband on our wedding day. I...didn't think I'd be tempted to break my vow so soon."

He stood and stared at her, and then shoved one hand in his pocket, the other hand still holding the gift that he had so thoughtfully gotten for her. It was small, maybe jewelry? Surely not a ring. Certainly they were too young for anything like that.

"Do you promise that you won't kiss anyone else?" he asked softly.

"I do. You're the only one I want to kiss. I sometimes dream about that."

He smiled wide, and then, so softly she almost didn't hear, he said, "Me too."

Her eyes searched his face. Did this mean that there was more to their relationship than him protecting her at school from the bullies that had been after her, holding her hand between classes, and pretending to be her boyfriend?

She smiled back at him, returning the expression on his face.

"If you promise that you won't ever kiss anyone else, that would be Christmas present enough for me. For now."

"I promise." The words fell easily from her lips. She didn't have any desire to kiss anyone else. Of course she was going to promise that.

"I wanted to ask you to be my girlfriend for real. But I don't want to get you in trouble."

She pressed her lips together. She wanted to say yes with all of her heart. "My parents don't want me to have a boyfriend. They want me to do this courtship thing, that you only do when you're ready to actually get married. They said the idea of having a boyfriend before you could actually do the married thing was silly."

"I don't like to hear that, but your parents are right. It's just not what everyone else does."

"I know." She looked down at the snow, sad, because he would probably want a girlfriend like everyone else. Then it occurred to her that she didn't have a promise.

"I don't know what's in the box, but I guess I would rather have a promise from you like the promise I just gave you for Christmas."

His brows drew down before another grin lifted his lips. "You want me to promise that I won't ever kiss any girl but you?"

She nodded.

"I promise."

Her heart felt like it would swell so big it would burst.

"And that is my second gift. Here. This is my first. I mean for you to have it."

"But I don't have two gifts for you," she said, even as her fingers reached out to take the little box from his hand.

"I like that I gave more. I think that's the way it should be. The man should always give more."

She glanced up in the process of pulling the ribbon and carefully unwrapping the little package. Inside was a jewelry box as she had suspected, and she was almost dying of curiosity to open the lid and find out what it was.

She carefully tucked the paper in her pocket, so it wouldn't blow away, and then after glancing at him and seeing he was looking down at her with a concentrated expression on his face, she looked back at the box and opened the lid.

The moon was light enough that she could see the sparkle reflected off the plain gold cross nestled in the dark blue velvet.

"Oh, it's so pretty," she breathed as she touched it with one bare finger.

"I wanted to get you something. I've been trying to figure out what for a long time, but nothing seemed to fit. Not until I saw that. I know it's not romantic, but it seemed to suit you, and... I hope you like it."

"I love it. I'll wear it all the time. Thank you so much." She couldn't believe that he had thought to get her something, and she loved that it was something that suited her personality so well. He knew what was important to her, and he also knew that she didn't like a lot of fancy things, and she loved that the cross was just plain and perfect.

"Can I help you put it on?" he asked, sounding hesitant.

"Please?" she said.

He grabbed a hold of one of his gloves with his teeth, pulling it off, then grabbed the other glove and yanked it off before sticking them in his pockets.

"I might be too clumsy to open the clasp," he said as she handed him the box and he pulled the delicate gold chain out.

"I'll move my hair, but hurry because it's cold out," she said, shivering as a gust of wind blew snow and ice crystals into her face.

"I don't want to keep you out much longer. But... Christmas vacation seemed like forever without seeing you at all."

"I might be in trouble if my parents thought that I planned to meet you here."

"I don't want to get you in trouble. But I do appreciate you coming out." The delicate gold chain was cold against her neck as he put it around, and she lifted her hair so he could clasp it in the back.

"There. It's almost as pretty as you are."

She let her hair fall back down and used one finger to touch the chain on her neck.

They stood looking at one another, the moonlight making the snow glisten and the night feel surreal.

Finally she said, "I better get back inside. The kids are all sleeping, but if one of them wakes up and needs me, I need to be there."

He nodded. "Merry Christmas, Mina."

"Merry Christmas, Nash."

"Don't forget the present you gave me," he said, lifting a hand up, touching her shoulder before shoving it back in his pocket.

How could she forget? She gave him a promise, and she meant it. "Don't forget your other present too."

He grinned and shook his head. "I won't forget."

Most of her wished he would kiss her, but there was a part of her that really wanted to wait. Even though the need to step closer and touch him was almost overwhelming.

"I better go. It's a long walk home."

"You walked?" she said, blinking her eyes.

He nodded. "I'm hoping to save up to buy a car, but for now, it's the good old shoe leather."

He gave her one last smile, and a bit of a longing look, and then turned and walked out across the snow.

She couldn't believe he walked the whole way from his house to here, just to give her a necklace and to see her.

She waited until he was completely out of sight before she walked back inside, practically frozen and realizing he had to be even colder, but he had done it for her. It made her heart happy.

Chapter Thirty-One

"It has to be the best Christmas I've ever had," Tosha said as she closed the door quietly to the girls' room.

Tobias had come out of the boys' room just a bit before and now stood at the top of the steps, leaning a hip against the banister, his arms folded over his chest. "I could say the exact same thing. I can't remember a better one."

They smiled at each other, and then he held out a hand. She gladly slipped her fingers into his and thought about the day. They'd opened the gifts they'd gotten the children that morning, and Tosha had a hard time feeling like that day was reality. She actually had money to buy more than one gift per child. They hadn't gone overboard, but each of their kids had gotten several gifts for the first time. Then, they'd gone to Sweet View Ranch and spent the rest of the day with Tobias's family. It was happy chaos with his twelve siblings and all of their spouses, plus nieces and nephews running around, everyone happy and laughing. There was plenty of food, plenty of fellowship, and plenty of laughter. There were even a few odd strays, like Agathe and her husband Jim, and the maid who had been employed with the Clybourn family for years.

And of course Stonewall who was as much a part of the family as Tosha was, maybe even more. He'd definitely been around longer.

"Do you think that Stonewall and Joanna will ever get together?" she asked as they walked down the stairs and into the living room where the Christmas tree shone brightly with gifts scattered throughout the room and a few pieces of paper that someone had missed the only sign of the happy gift giving that had gone on earlier that day.

"Do you think they are going to? They say they're just friends," Tobias said, sounding truly perplexed. Maybe it was just her imagination that the two of them would be perfect together.

He stopped at the couch. "Do you want to sit for a while and look at the tree?"

"I'd love to." She'd never get tired of sitting beside Tobias, his arm around her, her snuggled up to his side.

That's how they spent most evenings after they put the kids to bed since they'd visited his cabin and kissed for the first time.

Of course, in the evening, there was plenty of kissing going on too. Tosha had to admit she looked forward to it. Almost as much as she looked forward to snuggling up beside him and enjoying the feel of him beside her.

She thought maybe they'd moved on to a different subject, but as always, his thoughtfulness and consideration of what she thought and said surprised her.

"Do you think Stonewall and Joanna would be a thing?"

"They just seem so...comfortable together."

"Comfortable the way best friends are comfortable. That doesn't necessarily mean romance, does it?"

"Don't you think that your spouse should be your best friend?"

"I do. I want her to be. I'll do whatever I can to have that." His words, as always, warmed her to her very bones. She closed her eyes and said a short prayer of thanks to the Lord for giving her this amazing man. Someone who truly cared about her and went out of his way to make sure that their relationship was more than a surface one.

"Same. I feel the same way. I don't just want you to be my best friend, I think you are. I can't imagine anyone else that I feel more comfortable with or who I would rather be around."

"That's how I feel too."

"I guess the kissing isn't bad either. In fact, it's one of the best things and something I look forward to every evening." She'd gotten so comfortable with him, saying that didn't even feel awkward at all.

"That's good to hear. I think that was a compliment. So you managed to teach me to kiss after all."

"I think you always knew how."

He grunted, and the arm that was around her shoulder tightened, pulling her closer to him.

She fiddled with the crease on his pant leg. "I was kind of hoping I could move into your room tonight."

Her words were met with total silence, and the chest beside her quit moving. Like he had stopped breathing.

"You don't have to if you don't want to," he finally said. "But that's a pretty fantastic Christmas gift. The best one I've ever had."

"I guess I wasn't thinking about it as a Christmas gift, it's just something that I want, and I've been ready for a while, I just…needed to get up the nerve to say something."

"It took nerve?"

"Of course. You might have told me you didn't want me."

"Never. I would never say that."

She moved her hand, resting it on his leg and leaning her head against his shoulder.

"All of a sudden, I feel like I'm ready to be done looking at the Christmas lights."

She laughed, hearing the humor in his voice but knowing he was also serious. "I think I've looked at them enough too."

"You're ready for bed then, Mrs. Clybourn?"

"I am, Mr. Clybourn."

They laughed at the formal titles and then stood together.

He turned out the lights and checked the door while she went over and stood at the bottom of the stairs.

She wouldn't have guessed just a little more than a month ago that she would be here tonight, deeply and irrevocably in love with her husband, who happened to be the best man she'd ever met, a man of character and convictions, of integrity and honesty and loyalty, and she couldn't have picked out a better man if she tried. But she was sure of one thing. God had chosen her husband, and He had given him to her.

She would be thrilled to spend the rest of her life with him.

<u>Join Jessie's list and be the first to know about new releases and sales on her books!</u>
<u>Read A Cowboy's Perfect Match</u>, the next book in the Sweet View Ranch series featuring Stonewall and Johanna, best friends who have their hands full trying to dodge his mother's matchmaking attempts. Maybe a spontaneously uttered fake engagement will save the day? Rarely...

A Gift from Jessie

View this code through your smart phone camera to be taken to a page where you can download a FREE ebook when you sign up to get updates from Jessie Gussman! Find out why people say, "Jessie's is the only newsletter I open and read" and "You make my day brighter. Love, love, love reading your newsletters. I don't know where you find time to write books. You are so busy living life. A true blessing." and "I know from now on that I can't be drinking my morning coffee while reading your newsletter – I laughed so hard I sprayed it out all over the table!"

Claim your free book from Jessie!